ROMANOV REIGN

By: Danielle Grant

A Spinoff from Pretty Assassin: The Beauty Mark

Romanov Reign

By: Danielle Grant

Romanov Reign

Copyright © 2019 Danielle Grant

This is a work of fiction. It is not meant to depict, portray or represent any particular real persons. All the characters, incidents and dialogues are the products of the author's imagination and are not to be constructed as real. Any resemblance to actual events or person living or dead is coincidental and is not intended by the author.

Dedication

This novel is dedicated to everyone who has ever shared, bought, read, and reviewed my work. Your support is much appreciated. Thanks for all the love and support. I hope you enjoy the story.

Romanov Reign

Table of Contents

They say your first kill was the only one you'll ever remember vividly, but for Stepan Romanov that couldn't be any more false. Although his last homicide was six months ago, it replayed in his head every night. Tonight would be no different than the rest.

"I did not kill Joseph Marino. The man you promised to love and cherish til death do you part did."

When her one good eye widened with shock, he nodded his head. "Yes, that is correct sister. Your husband is the one who killed your lover not me."

Before she could open her mouth and plead for her life, he sent a bullet through the center of her head. Stepan stood there for a minute and stared at his sister's lifeless body. Just as he got ready to turn and walk away with his brother Alexei, Elise's lifeless body jolted from her seat and hovered over him.

"You will reap what you sow, Stepan! Romanov blood lasts forever!" She shouted in their native Russian tongue.

Stepan raised his gun once more and placed another bullet between his sister's eyes once again killing her. That dream immediately ripped Stepan from his slumber. His throat was dry, extremely dry. He threw his legs off the edge of the bed and stood to his feet. He sauntered down the stairs into the kitchen to grab a drink from the refrigerator. As Stepan closed the refrigerator door, he stared at a face he hadn't seen in years. The person stood before him dressed in all white with a small smile on their face.

"Cynthia?" He asked not believing his eyes. The love of his life stood before him looking just as beautiful as the day he first laid eyes on her. Only there was one problem with this moment. Cynthia had been dead for over twenty years.

"Stepan, my love you must not take these things lightly." She said in her soft spoken voice.

Stepan frowned a little. "Cynthia, what are you talking about? How are you here right now?"

Cynthia walked over to him and rubbed the side of his face. "I've always been here, my love. I swore to never leave your side and I haven't, but I had to come to you and warn you." She said.

"Warn me about what?"

"The worst is yet to come. Be wary of the company you keep and the things going on around you. Be sure to always protect the girls. Naya is so beautiful. You did well by giving her a family and good life. She's so precious and innocent. She has a spirit like Cori, which means she's a fighter as well." Cynthia smiled.

Stepan got ready to reach out and touch her as he took a step towards her, but Cynthia vanished just as quickly as she had come. He stood there confused. He had always been a man with everything under control, but at this moment he felt that he was losing all his bearings.

"Papa! Papa!" Naya ran into Stepan's bedroom at full speed yelling his name and jarring him from his two part dream sequence. Though they were just dreams, they felt realistic. He had the dream for a reason. He knew that he needed to heed his wife's warning.

"Papa, are you up yet?" Naya asked as she climbed onto the bed.

Stepan smiled at her beautiful face. "I am now, sweetheart. What is all the excitement about this morning?" He asked as if he didn't already know.

Naya smiled at her father. "Today is the day that Cori is coming into town. Did you forget already?"

"Oh, I think I forgot all about that." He said with a straight face.

She smacked her hand over her forehead and shook her head. "Cori said that you might forget because you're getting old. That's why she put me in charge of taking care of you and making sure you don't forget important stuff."

Stepan snatched her up and started a tickle assault on her. Her laughs and giggles were so contagious that you couldn't help but laugh along with her. "You and your sister are going to stop calling me old." He said as he tickled her.

"Bu... but... but you are old, papa." She said between giggles.

"I'm not going to stop until you say what I want to hear." He told her.

Naya was laughing so hard her stomach started to ache. "Ne... never!" She shouted.

"Okay then you asked for it." He stopped tickling her stomach and grabbed her tiny feet and started tickling them.

"Okay... okay, I'll say it!"

He stopped and smiled as he watched her sit up on the bed. "Let's hear it." He folded his arms across his chest.

"You're not old... just a little ancient." She said and then jumped off the bed.

Stepan just stood there and laughed. "You act so much like Cori it's scary. Did you wash your face and brush your teeth?" He asked.

"Yes and nanna made breakfast." Naya replied.

"Okay, I'll be right down after I take a shower and get dressed."

"Okay." Naya skipped out of the room and closed the door behind her.

Stepan walked into the bathroom and stood in front of the mirror. He stared at his reflection for a moment.

"What or who am I supposed to be wary about? What's about to happen that my dead wife had to come to me in a dream and warn me?" He asked himself.

All he could do was make sure he stayed on alert and keep his eyes open for danger. Until it made itself known there was nothing he could really do. For now his focus was on spending time with his family and preparing for his niece's wedding. Anything else would just have to wait.

~*A few hours later*~

"They'll be here any minute now!" Naya yelled with excitement as she rushed down the hallway towards the stairs.

"Naya, calm down sweetheart and stop running before you hurt yourself." Sarah, Naya's nanny said.

Naya stopped in her tracks when she made it to the staircase. She then walked slowly down the stairs with Sarah right behind her. As soon as her feet touched the landing she took off running again.

"Naya!" Sarah yelled after her as she followed her.

"Naya Romanov!" A voice called out causing her to halt all movements.

She turned to find her father staring at her with a disapproving look. "Naya..."

"Yes daddy?" She gave him a smile that usually works in her favor, but the look he gave her let her know it wasn't working this time.

"Why are you giving Sarah a hard time and not listening to her?" He asked.

She shrugged her shoulders and stared down at the floor. Stepan walked over to her and lifted her chin up so that she was looking up at him. "Listen sweetheart, I know that you're excited to see your sister, but that doesn't mean when an adult tells you not to do something you don't listen to them. Do you understand?"

Naya nodded her head. "Yes daddy."

"Now apologize to Sarah."

She turned towards Sarah who was a few feet away from them. "I'm sorry Sarah, I won't do it again."

Sarah smiled at her. "Apology accepted sweetie."

Naya turned back around towards her father. "Can I go wait outside for Cori now?" She asked.

"No, but you can wait for her in the living room. You do know that there are other family members coming today as well, right?" He questioned with a half smirk. In a few days they would be celebrating a wedding within the family so there will be a house full of Romanovs walking around soon.

"Yes, but I just really miss Cori. Plus not everybody is nice..."

"Who isn't nice to you?" Stepan frowned.

Before Naya could respond the doorbell rang. Naya started jumping up and down. "She's here, she's here!" She shouted as she took off for the front door.

Stepan didn't bother to stop her once he saw that Maxim was already at the door. When Maxim opened the door Alexei and his wife Sofia stood on the other side.

"Uncle Alexei did you see Cori out there?" Naya asked as she looked around his tall frame.

Alexei smiled down at his niece as he scooped her up in his arms. "No, the plane hasn't landed yet." He told her.

"How about you and I go bake some cookies for when everyone arrive?" Sofia smiled at her.

"Double chocolate chip cookies?"

"Yes, we can make that and a few other kinds as well. Come on sweetheart."

Alexei kissed Naya on her cheek before he placed her down on her feet. As soon as he did she grabbed Sofia's hand and led her towards the kitchen. Sarah the nanny followed close behind them.

"Join me in my office." Stepan said to his brother.

Alexei patted Maxim on the shoulder as he walked passed him. A few moments later he strolled into his brother's home office and was handed a drink.

"With everything that's been going on in our lives the last six months we haven't really had time to talk." Stepan said as he took a sip of his drink.

"What is it that we need to talk about?" Alexei questioned.

Stepan shrugged. "Well for starters your only child is about to get married in a few days."

Alexei chuckled and then polished off the rest of his drink in one gulp. "Yes, my only child... my only daughter is about to get married to a woman."

"I thought that you approved of their relationship?"

"At first I honestly thought it was a phase that she was going through. Now I know that it is more serious than I thought." He admitted.

Stepan nodded at his brother in understanding. He too thought that his niece Alyona was just going through a phase until he actually saw them interact with each other.

"From what I could tell, Alyona and Monica truly love each other. Seeing her happy is what's most important, isn't it?" He asked.

Alexei sighed. "Of course I want my daughter to be happy. I just assumed someday that I would have grandchildren."

"They could always adopt children, Alexei."

"But they won't have the Romanov blood coursing through their veins." He argued.

"Does that make them any less family? Naya doesn't have my blood running through her veins, but that doesn't make her any less my daughter than Cori. Sometimes it isn't just blood that makes you family."

"You're right, brother. When I look at Naya, I see her as my niece. I love her just as much as you do."

"Then isn't it possible that you could love any child that Alyona would bring into the family?"

"I believe so... you seem to be in good spirits about all of this." Alexei gave him a raised eyebrow expression.

Stepan chuckled a little. "Well, after what happened with Cori in that explosion, I realized that may be an only option for her and Will."

"Adoption?"

Stepan nodded. "Yes, the doctor said that she might not be able to have children of her own someday. I'm just keeping an open mind and you should too. Alyona senses your disapproval of her and Monica getting married."

Alexei glance over at him. "She talked to you about it?" He asked.

"Yes, she did. She's worried that you will disown her and not walk her down the aisle."

"Nonsense, she's my little girl. She knows that I love her."

"Maybe you should tell her and remind her of that."

"You're right; I'll talk to her once she arrives."

"Good..." Stepan replied as he got lost in deep thought.

"What is troubling you, brother?" Alexei asked grabbing his attention again.

"I've been having the dream again."

"The dream of Elise's death?"

"Yes, but this time it was different. Cynthia also came to me last night... well this morning. They were both warning me."

Alexei leaned forward in his seat. "What type of warning?"

"In the dream Elise threatened that I would reap what I sow and something about Romanov blood." He replied.

"What did Cynthia warn you about?"

"She basically warned me not to take what Elise said lightly and that I needed to watch everyone around me. It wasn't the first time I dreamed about my deceased wife, but it was the first time it felt real."

"Then that means we need to heed her warning. I've been feeling as if something was coming. That dream was a sign." Alexei said.

"We'll stay alert, but for right now I think we need to focus on our family. We have a wedding to prepare for."

"In that case I'm going to need another drink." They both chuckled as Alexei stood to refresh both of their drinks.

~~~~~~~~~~~~~~~~~~~~~~~~~~~~~~

~An hour later~

As soon as the car pulled up in the large circular driveway, the front door opened up. Maxim stepped out of the house and walked the short distance to the car. He opened the back door and reached out a hand to help the ladies out of the car.

"Thanks Maxim, it's good to see you again." Alyona said and kissed him on the cheek.

"It's good to see you as well." He said before he helped Monica, Katara, and Heidi out of the car next.

"Are my parents here already?" Alyona asked.

"Yes, they arrived an hour or so ago." Maxim replied.

She exhaled loudly and looked over at Monica. "Well, let's go say hi." She said as she grabbed her hand. Katara and Heidi followed close behind them.

Maxim leaned down and glanced into the car. Cori smiled back at him while she held her finger up for him to give her a minute. He nodded and then closed the door.

"So, when will you be heading to the airport?" Cori asked with her cell phone pressed against her ear.

"Right after I finish this meeting I'm heading straight to the plane. It's not like you miss me anyway." Will teased.

She blushed. "Yeah, you're right I don't."

"Oh damn, it's like that?"

"Yup." She giggled.

"Well I might as well stay my black ass here then."

Cori frowned. "You better not even think about it. You're my date to the wedding."

"Is that all I am?" He asked.

A smile spread across her face again. She's been doing that a lot when she's around or talking to Will. He always kept a smile on her face.

"No, you're my maintenance man too." She started laughing when she heard him gasp on the other end.

"Why you do me like this baby? I thought you loved me but all you do is abuse and mistreat me." Will said.

"You know I love you."

"You better... Look baby, I have to go. I'll see you later when I get there." He told her.

"Okay."

"I love you."

"I love you too." She ended the call and then climbed out of the car. When she did Maxim was waiting there for her.

"Hello Cori." He greeted her.

"Hey Maxim, it's good to see you." She greeted him with a hug.

"Your sister is anxious to see you." He told her.

"I'm anxious to see her too." She said as she made her way inside the house.

As soon as Cori made it through the front door she was rushed by an excited Naya. Cori leaned down and picked her up. Naya wrapped her arms around her neck and gave her a tight hug.

"You're finally here! Daddy didn't even remember that you were coming today, but I did." Naya said with a big smile plastered on her face.

"Of course he didn't, remember I told you he's getting old." Cori joked.

"I heard that." Stepan said as he strolled down the hallway to where they were standing.

Cori smiled over at her father. "Hey daddy."

"Hey sweetheart." He greeted her with a kiss on the cheek.

Stepan glanced around before he placed his attention back on the girls. "Where is Will?" He asked Cori.

"Yeah, where is he? I want to show him my pretty dress for the wedding." Naya said as she looked behind them at the door.

Cori chuckled at her excitement to see Will. She loved when he came around because he spoiled her rotten. Add that to the fact she had a little crush on him.

"He'll be coming in a little later. He had some business to attend to first." She responded to their question.

"Oh okay, well I'll let you get settled in and then we could catch up." Stepan said before he turned on his heels and headed back to his office.

Naya looked at Cori and gave her a bright white smile. "Are you going to help me unpack?" Cori asked her.

"Yes, but first we have to grab some of the cookies that me, Aunt Sofia, and Sarah made."

"Did you make our favorite?"

"Yup, double chocolate chip." Naya said with a nod.

"Well, we better go get some before the rest of the family arrive and eat them all." Cori said and then headed towards the kitchen after she placed Naya down on her feet.

~~~~~~~~~~~~~~~~~~~~~~~~~~~~~~~~

~Later that night~

Cori walked around her childhood home as memories of her as a child floated through her mind. She couldn't stop the smile that graced her face as she thought about the time she and Alyona got caught sneaking the liquor infused chocolate that her father hid in the back of the pantry. They got grounded for two weeks, but was able to get their sentenced drop down to a week after buttering up to their fathers. Cori found herself laughing out loud at that memory.

"What are you out here laughing at?" A voice said from behind her.

Cori turned around to find her cousin Alyona walking towards her. "I was just thinking about the time we got caught eating the liquor infused chocolate."

Alyona laughed. "We were sick for days after that, but now as adults it's one of our favorite candies."

"Yeah, it is." They were quiet for a minute. Cori noticed that something had been bothering Alyona. Since they were alone now was a better time than any to find out what it was.

"Let's go for a walk in the backyard." She suggested.

"Okay."

Once they made it out the back doors and started their walk, Cori glanced over at Alyona. She looked like she was in deep thought.

"Alyona, now it's just you and me. Tell me what's been going on with you lately?"

Alyona looked over at her as she wrapped her arms around herself. "What do you mean?"

"Lately, you've been walking around like you got something heavy on your mind. You can talk to me about anything..."

"I know that." Alyona cut her off.

"Okay, then tell me what's been bothering you? Is it about the wedding?" Cori asked.

"Yes and no."

"Are you having second thoughts about marrying Monica?"

"No, of course not. I love her."

"Then spit it out and tell me what's going on with you."

Alyona sighed. "I don't think my father approve of me marrying Monica."

Cori frowned at her. "What would make you think that? I thought he gave his blessing?"

"He did or at least I thought he did. It just seems like every time my mother or I mention the wedding he walks away like he don't want to hear or think about it. Cori, I love my father. You know I do, but I also love Monica too and I don't want to have to choose between the two of them. It would break my heart." She cried.

Cori pulled her into her arms and hugged her tight. "Alyona, you know uncle Alexei loves you. You are one of the most important people in his life. He would do anything to make sure you are happy. I think you should talk to him about how you are feeling. You should do it before the wedding."

Alyona pulled away and wiped the tears from her face. "You're right; I need to talk to him. I'm just scared that he may say what I don't want to hear."

"Well, at least you would know the truth and then you'll be able to move accordingly going forward."

"Yeah, you're right. How did you become so wise?" Alyona smirked.

"I've always been this way." Cori pushed her in the shoulder.

"Uh no, I think Will is brushing off on you." Alyona joked.

"Oh whatever. Speaking of Mr. Cooper, he should've been her already." She checked the time on her watch.

"Maybe he got caught in traffic."

"Let's head back in so I can call him."

They walked the short distance back to the house. After stepping inside Cori made sure the doors were locked and secured. She and Alyona then made their way to the front of the house where the stairs were. They told each other goodnight as they went their separate ways to their bedrooms.

Cori opened her bedroom door and walked inside before locking it behind her. She was about to walk over to her phone where it sat on the nightstand charging, when she heard a noise come from inside her bathroom. Cori reached for the switchblade in her back pocket that she kept close to her at all times. She crept over to the door and right when she made it in front of it, the door opened up. Cori threw the switchblade, but instantly regretted it when she saw who it was on the other side of the door.

Will reflexes caused him to move out of the way just in time before the blade was able to hit him. He turned his head slightly and watched as the blade hit the bathroom wall. He then turned back around to face his woman.

"Damn, I know I was running a little late, but did you really have to try and kill me for it?"

"Baby, I'm so sorry. I didn't know it was you in there."

"Who else would it be that you'll need a weapon for? This place is locked down like fort Knox." He told her while still looking at her funny.

"You never know someone could have snuck in here to kill me." Cori said with her arms folded across her chest.

Will laughed at her statement. "They'll have a better chance going after the president than coming for your pretty ass." He said as he pulled her close to him.

"Did you miss me?" He asked as he pecked her softly on the lips.

"Yes, a little bit. What took you so long? You we're supposed to be here an hour ago." She said.

"I know, but that business meeting took longer than I expected it to. Maxim let me in and showed me to your bedroom." He replied.

"Is everything okay now?"

"Yeah, it's good now. So, what did I miss?" He pulled her in closer.

"Nothing really, your best friend was waiting for you though. She wanted to show you her dress that she's wearing to the wedding." She chuckled.

Will grinned. "You sound a little jealous, baby."

She rolled her eyes. "I have nothing to be jealous about."

"Yeah, if you say so. I wanted to take a shower before bed, you care to join me?"

"I already took my shower." She replied.

"That's okay I can dirty you back up." He said before he pulled her into the bathroom and closed the door.

Cori and Will spent half the night getting reacquainted with each other. By the time they finally decided to get some sleep they were both exhausted. Sleep fell upon them easily.

~~~~~~~~~~~~~~~~~~~~~~~~~~~~~~

The following morning there was a small knock on the bedroom door. Will turned over to find that he was alone in bed. He heard the water running in the bathroom and figured that's where Cori ran off to. He climbed out of bed and threw on his pajama pants and a robe. The knocks on the door sounded again. He made his way to the door and unlocked it before he opened it. He smiled at who he found standing there.

"Will, you're here!" Naya yelled with excitement.

"Good morning, pretty girl." He greeted her.

Naya blushed. "Good morning. Where is Cori?"

"She's in the bathroom right now."

"Oh, are you going to come and eat breakfast with us?" She asked him right as the bathroom door opened and out stepped Cori.

"Good morning, Cori." Naya greeted her.

"Good morning, princess. What are you doing up this early?" Cori asked as she walked over to the bed to put her socks and shoes on. She had gotten dressed in the bathroom after she got out the shower. She didn't want to wake Will up, but it looked like she was too late.

"I always wake up this early. Sometimes daddy take me with him on his run." Naya replied.

"Oh okay, well why don't you go put on your clothes and shoes so that you can go running with me this morning."

"Really?"

"Yes, now go and I'll be in there shortly."

"Okay." She turned to make a run for her bedroom, but then stopped and turned back to face them.

"Will, are you coming with us too?" She asked with an innocent smile.

Will chuckled at the look Cori made. "No, I'm not coming on the run with y'all. I will eat breakfast with you when you come back though." He told her.

"Yay! Okay, let me go get ready." She ran down the hallway.

"Naya, walk don't run!" Cori yelled after her.

Will closed the door and then turned around to face her. "How long have you been up?" He asked her.

"Not very long, an hour maybe."

"I don't think I'll ever get used to your sleep pattern."

"You know I have to get my morning workout routine in." Cori said. She's been on a break from her assassin duties since she was released from the hospital six months ago. She needed to keep in shape and stay on her game because soon that break would be over and it would be back to work as usual.

"Yeah, I know. I'm about to take a shower." Will told her and kissed her on the cheek on his way to the bathroom.

Cori walked out the room and headed to Naya's bedroom. When she opened the door and glanced around the room. It was fit for a princess.

"I'm almost ready." Naya said as she put on her shoes.

Cori looked her over and giggled a little at what she had on. "Naya, sweetie you can't wear that to run in."

Naya looked down at her outfit and then back up at her sister. "Why not? Daddy lets me wear what I want when I go running with him."

Cori chuckled and shook her head. "That's because you have the daddy's little girl effect on him. He can't really say no to you. But as your big sister, I can't let you wear that outside."

"But why?"

"Well, because for starters it doesn't match. You have a dress on with rain boots." She told her.

"Well, I wanted to look pretty while I run and I need the rain boots because it might rain." Naya argued her case.

"Rain boots aren't good shoes to run in though, sweetie."

"What am I supposed to wear then?" Naya folded her arms across her chest.

"How about I find you something to wear. I know you have some type of workout clothes in here. I remember buying you some a while back." Cori replied as she walked over to her closet.

"I can't fit those anymore. I'm getting too fat." Naya complained.

Cori whipped her head around and looked at her. "Why would you say that?"

Naya shrugged her shoulders. "That's what Sasha says when she can't fit any of her clothes anymore."

Cori fought to roll her eyes at the mention of her cousin Sasha who was also Elise's daughter. "Don't repeat things that Sasha says. She's not that bright."

Naya giggled. "That's not nice to say."

Cori sighed. "You're right that wasn't nice. I meant what I said though. Stop listening to what she says. You are beautiful and there isn't anything wrong with your size.

You're just growing up fast and you know what that means, right?"

"No, what?"

"That means that we need to go shopping for you some more clothes." Cori smiled at her.

Naya jumped up off the floor. "Yesss! Can we get new shoes too?"

"Of course we'll get new shoes. We can't buy new clothes without getting new shoes as well."

Cori looked through her closet and found a pair of leggings and a t-shirt for Naya to put on. After she helped her change clothes she found her tennis shoes and put them on her feet. Once they were done they headed downstairs and out the back door.

Back in the house Alyona was headed in the kitchen to make some coffee when she spotted her father at the table reading the newspaper.

"Good morning, father. I didn't know you and mom stayed all night." She greeted him as she grabbed a coffee cup and poured her some coffee.

"Good morning, sweetheart. Yes, your mother was too tired to go home last night so we stayed. I'm glad that you're up, I wanted to talk to you." Alexei said as he folded the newspaper back and placed it on the table.

Alyona grabbed her coffee and walked over to the table and sat down. "Okay, what do you want to talk about?" She asked a little nervous.

"I want to talk about you and the wedding." He replied.

She took a sip of her coffee and swallowed hard. "Okay."

"It was brought to my attention that you are worried about how I feel about you marrying Monica."

"Yes, I am."

"Alyona listen, I will not lie and say that when you first announced to your mother and I that you were dating a woman that I wasn't shocked. At first I thought that it was just a phase you were going through. Then I noticed how you two are around each other. I can see the love she has for you and the love you have for her. My own selfish thoughts wouldn't allow me to be happy for the two of you at first. I was busy thinking about the legacy of the Romanov name when I should've been thinking about how happy you are. I'm sorry for making you feel that I don't care because I do. Monica makes you happy and that's all I ever wanted for you. I hope you can find it in your heart to forgive me."

Alyona jumped up out of her seat and rushed over to him. She wrapped her arms around his neck and hugged him tight. "Of course I forgive you daddy."

"I love you, sweetheart." Alexei told her as he returned her hug.

"I love you too."

Alexei was the first to pull away from the embrace. "Now, enough of this emotional mess. You have a wedding to prepare for in a few days." He said as he smiled at her.

Alyona was happy that she was able to get that off her chest and find out how her father truly felt. It felt as if a huge weight had been lifted off her shoulders. Now she could really focus on her special day. She wanted it to be perfect. After talking to her father she was now on cloud nine. In her eyes nothing could ruin her mood now.

~*The wedding day*~

Katara stood over Alyona adding the final touches to her face for her big day.

"Katara, you better not be painting my face to look like no damn clown. You've been at this for over an hour." Alyona groaned with her eyes closed as she sat in anticipation.

"I'm not going to lie to you cousin, you are giving me Ronald McDonald vibes right about now." Cori teased causing everyone in the room to erupt with laughter.

After a few moments, Katara stepped back from Alyona and handed her a mirror. Slowly, Alyona opened her eyes and saw what Katara had done. Her makeup was simple yet elegant; a gold and pastel pink coated her lids while precisely arched brows hovered over her eyes. Those porcelain dolls on TV didn't hold a candle to how breathtaking Alyona looked at that moment.

~Knock, knock~

Instinctively, Cori put a finger up to her lips and shushed everyone in the room while she opened the door where Monica stood.

"How may I help you, Monica?" She asked with a small smile.

"Well, I was just coming to check and make sure everything was okay in here. Heidi had just finished my makeup and..."

"Nope..." Cori shook her head while she cut her off.

Monica frowned and looked at her confused. "What?"

"You're not slick at all, Monica. You two brides cannot see each other before the wedding."

A smile graced Monica's beautiful face. "I thought that only worked for a bride and a groom, not two brides." She joked.

"Nope, it works for the two of you guys too. You look beautiful by the way. Heidi did a great job with your makeup."

"Thank you... I just wanted to check on Alyona and..."

"I'm not having second thoughts and you better not be either!" Alyona yelled from inside the room.

Monica chuckled but also released a sigh of relief. "Of course I'm not having second thoughts and it's good to know that you aren't either!"

"Ladies, it is time for you both to put your dresses on. The wedding ceremony starts in exactly forty-five minutes." The wedding planner clapped her hands and ushered Monica back to the room she was in to get dressed.

Cori closed the door and turned to face her cousin. "It's almost time..."

"I'm ready." Alyona said with a smile.

"Well, let's get that dress on you then." Sofia told her daughter as she smiled at her.

Outside near the garden all the guest were seated and waited anxiously for the wedding to begin. Stepan and Alexei stood back and watched as their family along with Monica's family came together.

"Are you ready to walk your daughter to her future?" Stepan asked him.

Alexei turned towards him and nodded. "Yes, I'm ready. I wasn't sure of their union at first, but now I know for a fact it was meant to be. They love each other and I love my daughter enough to make sure she's happy." He responded as the music started to play.

Stepan patted him on the back. "It's time brother." He said before he walked over toward his seat.

Alexei stood and observed all the bridesmaids walk down the aisle in their beautiful lavender dresses. He then watched as Monica walked with her father by her side. She had on a white mermaid style dress with a veil covering her face. Alexei turned around when he heard someone clear their throat. He stood there for a few seconds in utter shock at how gorgeous Alyona looked.

"How do I look?" She asked with a nervous giggle.

"You look absolutely breathtaking."

"Thank you, daddy."

He held his elbow out for her to grab a hold of. "Shall we?"

Alyona wrapped her arm around his. "Yes, we shall."

Even with the veil covering her face, Alexei could tell that his daughter was nervous. "Relax sweetheart, today belongs to you and Monica. There is nothing to be nervous about." He spoke in Russian.

She smiled at him as he led her to the woman she planned to spend her life with. Alyona and Monica stood in front of their entire family and expressed their love for each other. It was so beautiful that most of the older women couldn't help but shed a few tears. After the ceremony everyone moved to the other side of the large backyard under a huge tent where the reception was being held.

"I'm so happy for you guys." Cori gushed as she hugged both Alyona and Monica.

"Thanks Cori." Monica replied.

"You're next cousin." Alyona smirked.

Cori rolled her eyes. "I'm not in a rush for the whole marriage thing."

"So, if Will dropped down to one knee right now you wouldn't accept his proposal?" Monica questioned. Alyona awaited her answer because she wanted to know what her response would be too.

"I didn't say all that. Of course I would accept it. I'm just saying that I'm not rushing him. When the time is right then it would happen." Cori said. Right after the words left her mouth Will walked over towards them.

"Hello ladies." He greeted them with a perfect smile.

"Heyyy Will." Alyona and Monica said in a dramatic tone to tease Cori.

"Congratulations on the nuptials, ladies."

"Thank you." They both said at the same time.

"Do you mind if I steal her for a moment?" He asked as he nodded towards Cori.

"No, go ahead she's all yours." Alyona said with a grin on her face before she grabbed Monica's hand and led her away to mingle with some of the other guest.

Cori turned to her man. "Did I tell you how handsome you looked today?"

Will chuckled. "No you didn't, I was starting to think I looked like a bum to you or something."

"Never." She leaned up and kissed his lips.

"You look gorgeous in that dress." He complimented.

"Thank you, Mr. Cooper." She blushed.

There was a short pause of silence between them and Cori noticed that Will was stalling. "What's wrong?" She asked.

"Why does something have to be wrong?"

"Well, maybe because you're stalling."

Will sighed. "I have to leave in a few hours. Something happened at one of the warehouses and I need to go check it out."

"I want to be mad, but I know it's business so I can't. We were supposed to stay here a few more days together."

"I know baby and I'm going to make it up to you." Will kissed her lips.

Cori smiled up at him and shook her head. "You said that you have to leave in a few hours, right?"

"Yeah, what are you thinking about in that pretty head of yours?" He smirked at her.

"I'm thinking that maybe we could slip away from everyone and go do a few grown up things."

Will grabbed her hand and started to lead her back towards the house. Before they could make it to the doors, they were stopped by a small voice calling out to them.

"Cori and Will!" Naya shouted as she ran towards them.

Cori threw her head back and groaned. "We were so close." She mumbled.

Will laughed and squeezed her hand a little. Naya made it over to them with a big smile on her face.

"Hey pretty girl." Will greeted her.

Naya blushed and Cori shook her head with a slight chuckle. "Hey Will, can you be my dance partner?"

"I thought you were dancing with your father?" He asked.

"I was, but then uncle Alexei wanted to speak with him about something. So, can you dance with me, please?" She begged with her hands clamped together.

Will glanced over at Cori and gave her a half grin. "I can't turn a face like that down."

Cori giggled. "No, you can't. It wouldn't be nice."

"Yeah and I'm a very nice man." He winked at her.

"Yup, he's the nicest." Naya complimented with a head nod to help him out.

"Go, go dance with the princess."

Naya squealed and Will chuckled as he held his hand out for her to take. Cori stood there and watched as they made their way to the dance floor.

"You got ditched for your younger sister, huh?" Katara asked as soon as she walked over to her.

"Yeah, she's way cuter. You know they always go for the cuter sister." Cori joked.

"That sucks."

"Where did Heidi run off too?"

Katara shrugged as she looked around. "She was over there flirting with one of the guys on the staff."

They glanced at each other with raised eyebrows before they both laughed. They knew it was a possibility that Heidi was somewhere bent over.

"After that near death experience she is living her best life." Katara said.

"Yes and I don't blame her as long as she's careful."

"I thought I was going to come out here and find my Russian husband." Katara said with a roll of her eyes.

Cori laughed, but when she saw the look on Katara's face she knew she was being serious.

"You laughing, but I'm serious. I want to find someone to love me and start a family with."

Cori wrapped her arm around hers. "Love will find you when the time is right. You have to be patient."

"Yeah, I know."

A weird feeling overcame Cori. She glanced around and something seemed off to her. Her eyes then searched to where Will and Naya were at on the dance floor. She started to smile at them, but when she noticed a flash and then a red dot on Naya's dress; that smile got wiped away.

"Will!" Cori called out to him. She started running towards them.

Will glanced her way and frowned. He saw the look on her face, but had no time to register it. He noticed the flash and before Cori could make it to them shots rang out. Will's reflex was to protect Naya. He turned just in time before the bullet could pierce her. He ended up taking the shot to his back.

The guest started screaming and running for cover. Cori pushed through everyone to get to Naya and Will. A bullet flew pass her face, but she moved just in time before it could hit her. She glared at the gunman as she slipped her hand under her dress and removed two knives that were attached to her thigh. She threw one knife at the shooter that kept trying to shoot her. The blade ripped right through the center of his throat. Not once did Cori slow down or stop moving.

"Naya... Will, are you two okay?" Cori questioned when she finally made it over to them.

"Yeah, get her and get to safety." Will said as he pulled the gun out that was attached to his ankle.

"What about you?"

Will grabbed her face and brought it towards his. He brushed his lips against hers before kissing her. "I'll be okay just go and get Naya to safety. The bullet caught my vest."

Cori grabbed a crying Naya and held on to her tight. She still gripped the other knife in her hand. She and Will both stood up at the same. There were still a few active shooters. Two had their guns aimed at them.

"Go!" Will shouted.

Cori took off running with Naya in her arms. The two gunmen both turned their weapons towards them. That's when Cori realized that they were the targets.

Without any hesitation Cori released the knife in her hand. It landed directly in the forehead of the shooter. Will ended up taken care of the other shooter with a single shot to the head.

The gunfire lasted for only a few minutes. It ended just as quickly as it started. The end result was a yard full of dead bodies scattered throughout the grass. Will took notice that the shooters were all wearing the server's staff uniform.

"What the hell happened out there?" Alexei shouted at the men that were on the security detail for the wedding.

"I don't know, sir. Everyone was vetted before they were allowed entry on the grounds." One of the guards stated.

"Apparently, someone fucked up on that!"

"Who was responsible for vetting the staff for the wedding?" Cori questioned when she entered the room. They were down in the East part of the basement. It's where Stepan handled some of his business meetings.

"Anton was the one who vetted them."

Cori glanced around the room that was filled with huge scary men. Men that had been with her father's security team for years. She looked over at Maxim who stood beside her with a stone facial expression. Cori knew he was taking in every movement and facial expression that the other men made.

"Where is Anton?"

"He was one of the wounded."

A door being slammed shut caused everyone besides Alexei, Cori, and Maxim to look that way. Stepan entered the room with an angry facial expression. When he glanced at his brother his eyes softened a little.

Alexei tried to read his eyes. "What is it brother?"

"We took a few personal casualties."

"My wife and daughter?" He asked.

"They are safe and unharmed. We lost our mother in the gunfire."

That news caused Cori and Maxim to also turn his way. The head of the Romanov family had been gunned down on Romanov property. Russia was about to feel their wrath. The Romanov Reign was going to go down in history.

Chapter 4

Cori left her father and uncle in the basement to deal with the security team. She felt bad for her father and uncle more than anyone. Their mother meant the world to them. Cori knew that they were going to need time to deal with her death, but at the moment they didn't have any. She was also crushed to know that she would never see her grandmother again. Her death was going to hit the Romanov family hard, especially Naya. She spent most of her time with her and they were close. Whoever was responsible for her death had never felt pain like they're going to feel once their identity was revealed.

Cori got her bearings together before she made her way back upstairs. The first face she saw was Alyona's. She rushed up to Cori and embraced her in a hug.

"Did you hear about grandma?" Alyona asked her with tears in her eyes.

"Yes."

"What happened, Cori? I thought all the drama was over. Someone shot up my wedding reception." She cried.

"I'm just as clueless as you are, Alyona. We didn't have any problems with anyone else."

Alyona wrapped her arms around herself. "This was supposed to be the best day of my life. Now it will forever be known as the day I lost my grandmother."

"How are Monica and her family?" Cori asked.

"They had just left for the hotel. I told Monica that I would meet them there after I talk to you. Katara and Heidi had gone with them." She replied.

Cori placed a hand on her shoulder. "You know this family has been through tough times before. Grandma's death might be the hardest thing we've ever have to face. We've always managed to come off on top though. This won't be any different. We'll find out what happened today and take care of it. I'll call you with any updates, but you should be with your new wife right now. I'm sure Monica and her family will have questions."

"Yeah, questions that I don't have the answers to."

"There are some things they don't need to know. I know Monica is your wife, but that goes for her as well."

"Cori..."

"No Alyona, that could be life or death; for all parties." Cori stressed with a stern look.

Alyona slowly nodded her head. "Okay."

Cori pulled her into her arms and hugged her. Alyona returned the hug and laid her head on Cori's shoulder.

"I love you, cousin."

"I love you too. Where is Naya?" Cori asked her.

Alyona pulled away from her. "She's with Will at the moment. She won't let him out of her sight until she sees her papa." That caused her to smile for the first time since all the drama started.

"Let me go check on her. Are you going to be okay?"

Alyona nodded and gave her a small smile. "Yes, I'm going to head over to the hotel. I would ask my mom to come with me, but I know she won't leave without my father."

"That's true; get Maxim to take you to the hotel. Until we know what's going on your security detail will double." Cori let her know.

Alyona didn't bother to argue with that. She knew how her family was. She was already prepared for them to double security.

Cori made her way upstairs to Naya's room. She assumed that's most likely where Will would have taken her. She got to the door and twisted the knob. As soon as she opened the door she spotted Will with his hand on the gun in his waist. Behind him was a weeping Naya.

"It's okay baby girl, it's just your sister." Will told Naya.

Once she heard those words she rushed from behind him and over to her big sister. Cori picked her up and hugged her tight. She couldn't believe how close they came to losing her. That thought made her look over at Will. If it wasn't for his quick reflexes Naya might had been another loss for the family.

"Cori, where is papa? I want him." Naya cried.

"He's okay princess; he'll be up here in a minute." She replied.

"Okay." Naya laid her head down on her shoulder.

"I need to talk to you." Will said. He was texting on his phone so he wasn't looking up at her when he said it.

Cori walked over to Naya's bed and sat her down on. She then grabbed her headphones and IPad off of her nightstand.

"I want you to put these headphones on and watch something on your IPad while Will and I talk, okay?"

Naya nodded. "Then can you go get daddy?"

She smiled at her beautiful little sister. "Yes."

"Okay."

After she got her situated on her tablet, Cori walked over to Will. He stood over by the window. As soon as she was in arm's reach he pulled her into his arms. Cori embraced him back.

"Thank you for protecting her."

"You don't have to thank me for that. She's your family which makes her mine too." He replied with all seriousness.

"I don't know what's going on or who was responsible for that attack. It has to be someone that's not afraid to go to war with a Romanov." Cori said still clueless at what happened.

"They were aiming for you and Naya." Will told her.

She looked up at him even more confused. "I don't have any beef with anyone. Not anyone that I know of. Why would someone be crazy enough to come for me?"

"I don't know, but I noticed that most of the gunfire was aimed at the two of you."

She thought about it for a moment. "Do you think it has anything to do with the men involved with the sex trafficking ring? Maybe they were upset that I was involved with killing their supplier and freeing those little girls." That thought made her glance over at Naya. The little girl had already been through a lot and she was barely six years old.

"I don't know it could be, but I'm not sure. I do know that all the shooters were wearing a server's uniform. That had to be how they got in. They were..."

The sound of the door being opened caught both Will and Cori's attention. They both reached for their weapons as they stood in front of the bed to block Naya. They relaxed when they saw that it was Stepan at the door.

Stepan walked inside and closed the door behind him. He first walked up to Cori and pulled her in for a hug. Once Naya caught sight of him, she removed the headphones and rushed to him.

"Daddy!" She cried as she jumped into his arms.

"It's okay princess I'm here." He rubbed her back.

"It was a lot of shooting and people were screaming. I saw blood too, daddy."

"I hate that you had experienced that sweetheart."

"Are they the bad men that were coming to get me again?" She asked in a soft voice.

Stepan looked her in the eyes. "What are you talking about, angel?"

"You know, the bad men that took me the first time. Were they coming back to take me to that horrible place?"

Stepan glanced back at Cori. She stepped up and rubbed Naya on the back.

"Those men are no longer on earth, princess. Do you remember that I made sure they would never hurt you again?"

Naya looked like she was thinking about it. She then nodded her head. "Yes, I remember."

"Do you also remember that bad place lighting up like fireworks?"

She smiled. "Yes."

"No one is going to get to you. We won't allow it, okay?"

"Okay, sissy." Naya responded before she laid her head on her father's shoulder. Within a few seconds she was out for the count. She had a long exhausting day. Now that she laid eyes on her sister and farther she could fall victim to the sleep she had been fighting.

"What's the next move?" Will asked getting Stepan and Cori's attention.

"I have a favor to ask of you two." Stepan said as he looked between Cori and Will.

"Name it." Will replied.

"I need you to take Naya back to Chicago with you."

"You're worried that more shooters will come?" Cori asked.

"No, I'm sure no one will try that shit again after today. I just need her to be safe while I figure out who's responsible for all of this. You two are the best people to do that. I trust that you would protect her with your lives. You showed that already." He nodded at Will.

Cori had gone on to tell him about what her and Will were discussing before he walked in the room. Stepan told them that it could be a possibility, but they needed to make sure first.

"I'll look into that and find out for sure if it was them. Now that we know they were after you two, it has to be someone we recently pissed off." Stepan said.

"Everybody that we pissed off recently is already dead." Cori replied.

"Apparently, not everyone." He stated.

Cori nodded. "I'll pack her things." She walked over to Naya's closet and grabbed her Princess and the Frog luggage.

While she packed up some of Naya's things Stepan nodded for Will to follow him out of the bedroom. He still had Naya in his arms. She held on to him tight as she slept.

Will closed the door once he stepped out. "What do you need?" He asked.

"I know that you are a busy man with an organization of your own to run. All I ask is that you keep my girls safe. If whoever did this was brave enough to come on my property to kill them they had to be planning this for a while. They're going to strike again since they didn't get their main targets."

"You know that I'll protect them with my life. I'm going to be looking into some things on my end as well."

"Thank you."

"None needed..."

"Okay, I have her stuff ready." Cori said when she opened the door. She looked between her father and Will.

"I already have the plane ready. You can leave whenever you're ready, but I prefer it be soon." Stepan told them.

"Will Naya's nanny Sarah be coming as well?" Cori questioned.

"If that's okay with the two of you, then yes. She could help you out with Naya."

"That's fine with me." There was a short pause. Cori didn't know how to really ask her next question, but it had to be asked.

"Do you need help with making arrangements for grandma?"

Stepan sighed a little. "No, I'll take care of it and let you know the details."

She nodded and then walked up to her father. She wrapped her arms around him and Naya. "I love you, daddy."

"I love you too, my angel." He said in his native Russian tongue.

"Here, take your sister while I go explain everything to Sarah."

"I'll take her." Will stepped up and grabbed her out of his arms.

Stepan took one last look at them before he walked away. His thoughts were all over the place. The main one that kept him grounded was finding out who dared disrespect his family and end them in the most painful torturous way.

~~~~~~~~~~~~~~~~~~~~~~~~~~~~~

~A few hours later~

Stepan watched from the window as Will and Maxim assisted Sarah, Cori and Naya into the backseat of the town car. He would had driven them to the port himself but Cori was against it. She didn't want to risk them all being out and caught slipping. As the car slowly rolled off of the Romanov estate, Stepan kissed the crucifix he wore around his neck and said a silent prayer to the Heavens for the safety of Cori and Naya. He had already lost his mother; and he refused to allow another Romanov death happen. Especially not one of his girls.

Alexei walked up behind his brother and handed him a glass of Bourbon.

"You look like you could use this." He said as he took a swig of his own drink.

"Someone was bold enough to step foot onto my property and attack our family, Alexei. That was the boldest move to make."

"And also the dumbest. The name Romanov sends chills up spines from Moscow to the States so whoever did this must not mind dying a thousand deaths."

"Where are Alyona and Monica?" Stepan asked turning to face his brother.

"They went to a hotel with Monica's parents a little while ago."

"I owe my niece a sincere apology. This was supposed to be her wedding day not a bloodbath."

"Alyona understands that everything that happened here tonight was out of any of our control. She's not a kid anymore; she knows what kind of life her family leads."

"Yes, but Alyona has never been the one to thrill seek. That was always Cori; Aly's always been more reserved."

"Don't I know it?" Alexei forced a chuckle before he began speaking.

"But Alyona knows that her family only fights when necessary."

"I hope this doesn't cause any issues between her and Monica…"

"If she truly loves my daughter, brother, she will have to understand." A moment of silence fell between the Romanov brothers before they each swallowed and spoke next.

"What are we to do without our Matriarch?" Alexei asked with his voice almost in a whisper at this point.

"We do what she taught us to do; we find the sons of bitches who did this to her and we avenge her. Yuliya Romanov did not raise us to lie in wait. We take action now; especially since Will and Cori gave me a bit of info before they left."

"What was that?"

"Will said he noticed that the gunmen seemed to be aiming for Cori and Naya." Alexei's blood began to boil at the mention of someone intentionally trying to take out his nieces.

"The Ghost and The Grim Reaper is back, brother… Let's remind Moscow who the hell we are."

Chapter 5

The sound of wood being thrown against the wall and crashing to the floor could be heard throughout the building. The man who tossed the chair started to pace back and forth to calm himself down. His breathing was heavy, his fist clenched tight, and his face was twisted up in anger.

"This was a complete fucking disaster!" He shouted.

"Boss..." One of the other men that stood in the vacant building tried to speak.

He ignored the interruption and continued on with his rant. "All the hard work and time wasted within just a few minutes! We didn't even hit our targets! What the fuck happened out there?" He finally turned to face the five men that stood before him.

The men gave each other a look before they stared back at their boss. "We didn't expect the security team to be doubled what it originally was. We were outnumbered and..."

"Outsmarted! That's what the fuck you were. Now we're going to have to lay low for a while. They will be on full alert now."

The door being opened caught his attention. He turned and watched as his inside man made his way towards him. He took notice of his arm being in a sling.

"What happened out there today, Anton?"

Anton cringed at the way he spoke his name and glared at him. He knew that he was going to place the screw up on him.

"They doubled the security at the last minute. I had no time to warn anyone. We did take a few of them, but..."

"But what?"

"Yuliya Romanov got hit during the shooting. I got word that she didn't make it." Anton revealed in a nervous tone.

The man stood there with his eyes closed for a minute. "Are you telling me that none of you were able to kill Cori or Naya, but you killed the mother?"

"I didn't pull the trigger on that, but yes she was gunned down." Anton replied.

The man angrily chuckled. "Not only are they going to be pissed that someone brought gunfire on their property and ruined a family wedding reception. They are going to be on a fucking blood thirst rampage to revenge the death of their mother!" He shouted with his face turned a crimson shade of red. His plan for revenge wasn't going the way he had expected it to. He had been planning months for this attack and all his planning seemed to had been done for nothing now.

"This was supposed to be a smooth hit and you stupid son of bitches fucked that up! I had it all set up perfectly. The wedding was a good distraction. All you had to do was kill that bitch Cori and that little spoiled brat Naya! A woman and a child..." He shook his head and rubbed his temple with his thumb and finger.

"Maybe we got another chance now, boss." One of the other men that stood before him stated.

He looked over at him. "Oh yeah? How is that?"

"The mother's funeral could be a good day to strike again. They'll all be in one place and also be distracted. They'll be too busy mourning their loss to see us coming."

The man stared at him for a minute not saying a word. "Was it you?" He asked with his head tilted slightly to the side.

The confusion could be seen on his face. "Was what me?"

"Were you the one who killed Yuliya Romanov?" He questioned.

"No... no, it wasn't me."

The man nodded then looked at all of the other men. "Who was it that pulled the trigger that ended Yuliya Romanov's life?"

Thinking that he was about to be rewarded for being the one who spilled the blood of Stepan and Alexei Romanov's mother; the guy next to Anton stepped forward.

"It was me, boss. I killed the old bitch since I couldn't get to the other woman and child. I knew that her death would hurt them just as much as the other's." He smirked.

"I find it funny that you think what you did was a good idea."

"Wh... what?"

He pulled out a gun and shot him in the chest. "It wasn't a smart thing to do. It's only going to make our job harder to accomplish you stupid fucker!" He spat and then sent a bullet through his skull.

"Clean this mess up." He ordered before he walked out of the building. He had to come up with a better plan because no matter what he would have his revenge.

~~~~~~~~~~~~~~~~~~~~~~~~~~~~~~~~

Cori stared at Naya as she slept comfortably on the bed in the private bedroom on the jet. They had been in the air for a few hours so far. Naya had only woke up once and probably won't awaken again until the plane got ready to land.

Cori stood up and pulled the comforter over Naya's little body. Once she finished making sure Naya was good, she walked out of the room. She stopped where Sarah sat in one of the seats closest to the bedroom. The woman looked like she was fighting to keep her eyes open. Cori tapped her on the shoulder.

"Yes, Ms. Cori?" She glanced up at her.

"You don't have to call me Ms. Cori, Sarah. Cori will do just fine. How about you go back in the bedroom and get some rest with Naya?"

"Oh, thank you." Sarah said as she stood to her feet and walked towards the bedroom.

Cori then strolled over to where Will sat and took a seat beside him. He instantly placed a hand on her thigh. His eyes stayed glued to the phone that was in his hand.

"Things are going to be different with a kid in the house." She started.

Will finally place his phone down and gave her his full attention. "Yeah, I guess you can't be walking around the house naked anymore."

She giggled. "You wish I was walking around the house naked."

"I do, I really do." He chuckled.

"Stop looking so nervous at the thought of having her with us. We'll do fine; she already loves hanging with us." Will told her.

"I just don't want to mess this up. Naya needs stability and with my dad she had that. I'm just worried with everything going on and our schedules that we won't have enough time for her." Cori expressed.

Will put his arm around her shoulder and pulled her closer to him. "The good thing about being our own boss is that we set our own schedules. We'll move them around to fit Naya. You're worrying for nothing."

Cori looked up at his face with her head rested on his shoulder. "What about the business you needed to get back to and take care of?"

"I'll handle that once we land and you and Naya get settled at the house. I got Zel handling it for me at the moment."

"Well, if you need any help let me know."

He smirked and then kissed her on the head. "I'll let you know if I do. Look, if you're really worried about Naya's move with us talk to Tari."

"Talk to her about what? Tari has a boy not a girl."

"Yeah, but she knows more about kids then we do. Maybe she can give you some tips or advice."

Cori thought on it for a moment. "Okay, I'll do that."

They sat there quiet for a moment. They were both lost deep in their own thoughts. That was until Will broke the silence between them. "Do you want to talk about it?" He questioned.

"My grandma?"

"Yeah, I know you were close with her."

Cori smiled at the thought of her grandmother Yuliya. "She was the one who helped my dad raise me. She was the best grandma in the whole world."

"What type of woman was she?"

"She was a soft spoken, but stern woman. She never had to raise her voice to get her point across. When she talked everyone listened. My grandmother made sure that I knew how to be a lady." Cori chuckled.

"She would say in her native Russian tongue; Cori, you have to act more like a lady. Don't be a hard ass brute like your father and uncle. Ladies get more accomplished in what they're trying to get done because no one expects them to be anything but a soft vulnerable woman."

Will smiled. "That's the biggest mistake a man can make dealing with your little pretty ass."

Cori glanced up at him and batted her eyes. They both fell out laughing. "I'm going to miss her."

"Between your father, uncle, and our resources we'll find out who did this and end them."

"Mr. Cooper, I think I love you." She smiled at him.

"You think or you know?"

Cori pulled his face towards hers and kissed his lips. "I definitely know that I love you."

"You better because you ain't going anywhere." He pecked her on the lips a few times before getting comfortable in his seat. He and Cori decided to catch some shut eye before the plane landed back home.

~~~~~~~~~~~~~~~~~~~~~~~~~~~~

~Six hours later~

Cori gently tapped Sarah on the arm while shaking Naya awake at the same time. Sarah was the first to open her eyes since she was a light sleeper.

"We're getting ready to land so you have to be in a seat and buckled in." Cori said when Sarah's eyes landed on hers.

Sarah nodded and got up off the bed. When she went to help her wake up Naya, Cori told her she got it.

"Okay." Sarah replied before she walked out.

"Naya, time to wake up." Cori moved some of her curly hair out of her face. She smiled at how beautiful her baby sister was.

Naya slowly rubbed her eyes and opened them. She looked up at Cori and smiled. "Hi."

Cori giggled. "Hi, did you get some good sleep?"

She nodded. "Yes."

"Let's go get you buckled in your seat."

Naya accepted the hand that Cori reached out to her. She let her lead her out of the bedroom.

"Will daddy be coming out here with us too?" Naya asked Cori once they got to her seat.

"He might come to visit, but not to stay. He's going to be busy with work for a while."

"Is that why he sent me out here with you and Will?"

"Yes."

"Oh." Naya said and looked down at her hands as she twirled her fingers around.

Cori checked her seatbelt after buckling her in. She then looked at her and placed her hands on top of hers.

"What did you think he sent you out here for?" She questioned.

"Well, I thought that maybe he didn't want me anymore so he was giving me away." Naya said with her head down.

Cori lifted her chin up so that they were staring each other in the eyes.

"Naya, daddy loves you more than life itself. When you came into his life... no, our life it was for the better. You didn't just needed us, but we needed you too. Daddy would never give you away. He just wants to keep you safe and that's why he sent you with me."

"So, he still loves me then?"

"Yes, always and forever and ever." Cori smiled when Naya giggled.

"That means I was right and Sasha was wrong."

Cori frowned up her face a little. "What do you mean?"

"Sasha said that eventually my daddy will get tired of me and send me back to the bad men." Naya told her.

Cori tried hard to hide the anger that was burning up inside her. She and Sasha never got along as kids because Sasha acted too much like her mother Elise. She was selfish and inconsiderate of other's feelings and time. Cori didn't think that she was stupid enough to tell Naya those lies just to scare her.

"We're not going to listen to anything Sasha has ever said. She doesn't know what she's talking about. Sasha and I are going to have a little chat when I see her again."

"Okay."

"Baby, strap up we're getting ready to land." Will told Cori.

"Okay, babe." Cori took her seat next to Naya and buckled up. Thoughts of strangling Sasha with her bare hands floated through her mind as the plane prepared to land.

~~~~~~~~~~~~~~~~~~~~~~~~

Zel met Will and the Romanov group at the house ready to get to work. Will helped Sarah get settled in the guest room while Cori tended to Naya who was excited to be spending time with her big sister. After they got the both of them settled into their new living quarters, Cori met Will in the kitchen where he stood at the center island talking to Zel in whispered tones.

"Boss, I'll meet you in your office." Zel told Will and bowed towards Cori before he turned on his heels and made his way out of the kitchen. Cori watched him until he disappeared out of eyesight before she turned back around to face Will.

"He's loyal; I like him."

"I only keep solid ones around me, baby. You know that."

"I do…" He noticed that she was stalling and that was unusual for her.

"What's up with you, baby?"

"Can I talk to you for a second about what we discussed on the plane?"

"Yeah what's up?"

"With the lives that we both lead, do you think this is the safest place for Naya to be?" Will scrunched his face up as if she had four heads sprouting out of her neck before he answered her question.

"There is no better place for that little girl to be than with us. She's young and impressionable, but she's been through a lot. The one thing she needs especially after a night like today is consistency and to be around people she loves and trusts. That's us. I told you, if you want some advice, call Tari. You know she will come through."

"You know…" She began as she wrapped her arms around his neck.

"When you put things into perspective like that, it's really sexy." She smirked.

"Well, sometimes you just need a little reality check." He chuckled.

"Is Naya asleep?"

"No, I tried to tuck her in before I came in here, but she was wide awake."

"That's probably because she slept for most of the plane ride."

"Yeah, but I put a movie on for her and that should hold her attention until she fall back to sleep." Cori stated.

Will kissed her on the lips. "Cool; as soon as I get done talking to Zel, I'll meet you in the bedroom." He wiggled his eyebrows.

"You better bring that stamina with you." She rubbed her hands over the big print in his pants.

"You just better be ready for me." Will smacked her on the ass as she giggled and hurried out of the kitchen.

Will chuckled as he shook his head at her. He then walked down to his office where Zel was waiting for him. When Will strolled through the office door and closed it behind him, Zel had pulled up some information on his phone that he had for him.

"Alright, let me see it." Will stated after he took a seat behind his desk.

Zel pushed the phone to him and watched as he scroll through it. Will only scrolled for a few minutes before he passed him the phone back.

"What do you want to do about that, boss?" Zel questioned.

"You know how I feel about thieves. He's moving that shit on my territory without my permission. That means he's stealing from me. You know what happens when someone steals from me, Zel?"

The grin that spread across Zel's face almost made Will laugh. "They get sent home to meet their creator."

"Exactly. Set the meeting up for two days from now. I want this handled as soon as possible. I got other things that's of more importance than dealing with a thief."

"I'll get on that right after I leave here. What about that situation that happened in Russia?"

Will rubbed his chin. "For now I'm going to let Stepan and Alexei handle that. If they need our help then we'll lend it."

Zel nodded. "Is there anything else you need, boss?"

"Yes, I want you to put a team together to be on Naya's security detail. I want to make sure when Cori and I aren't around she's still safe."

"I thought Stepan usually have her travel with some of the guards from the Romanov organization?"

"After what just happened he felt it was best that I use my men until we find out everyone that was behind the shooting."

"I got you; I'll get on that immediately."

Will stood to his feet at the same time that Zel did. They walked out the office and headed to the front door. After Zel left Will locked the front door and set the alarm. When he made it upstairs he first checked on Naya. A smile broke out on his face when he saw her laid out on the bed with the comforter halfway on the floor. The light from the cartoon that she was watching lit up the room. He walked inside and pulled the comforter up over her body. He then turned the television off before he headed out of the room.

Seeing Naya made him want kids even more than before. He felt her being with them could be good practice for him and Cori. Even though the doctors told them that Cori may not be able to have kids, Will wasn't giving up hope. Plus, adoption was always an option too.

"I thought you'll never make it up here." Cori smiled at him when he walked into their bedroom.

"I didn't take that long." He said as he closed the door.

"You took long enough."

Will smirked and nodded towards the bathroom. "Come take a shower with me."

73

"Are you asking or telling me, Mr. Cooper?"

"I'm telling you now come on." He walked in the bathroom with a smirk on his face.

Cori threw her head back and laughed. "Not a lot of men get to live after trying to demand things from me." She said as she followed him inside the bathroom.

"I'm not a lot of men. I'm your man and as your man I want you to take a shower with me. I promise to make it worth your while." Will removed his clothes and tossed them in the hamper.

Cori eyed him from head to toe. "Well, that's one way to get me naked."

She watched as Will stepped inside the shower and turned the water on. "Are you coming in or are you going to watch me like a pervert?" He asked her.

Cori stripped out of her clothes and then climbed in the shower. Will turned around to face her. She watched as his eyes roamed her body from top to bottom.

"You're so fucking beautiful I get lost just looking at you sometimes." He said.

She walked up to him. "You make me feel beautiful from the way you look at me. I mean, I have had men tell me that I was, but it hits different when it comes from you."

Will pulled her to him. With their bodies pressed against each other, he used his other hand to brush some of her hair out of her face. "It hits different because it's coming from a man that loves you. A man that would do anything for you including laying down his life if that means protecting yours."

Cori dragged her hand down his abs and stomach to his rock hard dick. She gripped it tight and started to move her hand up and down its length.

"I think it's sexy as hell when you declare your love for me."

"You do?" Will bit down on his bottom lip to keep himself from moaning.

"Yes, I do. You know that it's mutual though, right?"

"The love part?"

"That too, but I was referring to the part about laying your life down for mine. You know I'll do the same in a heartbeat."

Will kissed her neck and then her lips. "I would rather you live for the both of us, baby." He whispered in her ear.

Cori was about to respond to that until Will lifted her up. He throw her up against the shower wall, wrapped her legs around his waist, and entered her.

"Mmmm..." She moaned as he stretched her out in a way only he could.

Will thrust deep inside her as he licked and kissed on her neck. He loved the way her pussy felt wrapped around his dick. It was tight, warm, and wet just the way he liked it.

"Do you remember what I said to you in the hospital after the bombing?" He asked as he moved in and out of her at a steady pace.

"Ye... yes!"

"I meant every word of it, baby. I'm not going anywhere and neither are you." He thrust inside her hard. He could feel her pussy muscles tightening up. That let him know she was almost at her peak.

Will pulled out of her and placed her down on her feet. Her legs wobbled a little, but he held on to her so she wouldn't slip. He turned her around so that she was facing the wall.

"Hold on, baby."

Cori placed her hands against the wall and waited to feel him back inside her. Will didn't disappoint when he thrust so deep inside her that she thought she could feel him in her stomach.

"Ooooh!"

Will gripped her hips as he pounded into her. He took his right hand and reached around to rub her clit while he continued to fuck her from the back.

"Shiiiiit! Ooooh Will, fuck me harder!" She moaned.

"You want me to go harder, baby?"

"Yessss!" She screamed out in complete bliss. Cori was glad that the bathroom was soundproof. She didn't need Sarah and Naya to hear them having sex.

Cori felt her legs about to give out on her. She spread her legs wider and kept her hands planted on the wall. Her body started to shake from the intense orgasm that ripped through her.

"Shit!" Will grunted as he emptied his seeds deep inside her. He kissed the back of her neck and then turned her around to do the same to her lips.

Cori smiled at him. "I love taking showers with you." She pecked his lips a few times.

He smirked. "I told you that I'll make it worth your while."

"You never disappoint, Mr. Cooper."

"I make it my mission never to do so, Ms. Romanov."

Will grabbed her body wash and washcloth off the rack inside the shower. He washed every inch of her body and made sure to be gentle when he washed between her legs. Will loved washing her sexy little body. It was something he enjoyed doing whenever they showered together. After he finished with her, he grabbed his own body wash and washcloth. While he washed himself up Cori rinsed the soap off of her body. Once they were done in the shower they got out and dried off. Will put on a pair of boxer briefs and silk pajama pants. Cori just put on some panties and a night shirt.

"Do you have a long day tomorrow?" She asked him once they were in the bed.

"No, I just got a few things to handle and I'm all yours." He replied.

"I want to go check on Alyona, Katara, and Heidi. I don't know if I should take Naya out of the house yet though." She told him.

"Why? If anyone can keep her safe it's you."

Cori laid her head on his chest. "You always know what to say."

"That's because I'm a genius. You really lucked up when you got with me." He joked.

"Go to sleep, Will. You always start to talk crazy when you are tired." They both laughed.

Cori snuggled closer to him as her eyes started to get heavy. Before sleep took her, she thought about her father. She prayed for his sanity for the upcoming battle they were about to embark on. She also prayed for the souls of the people that they planned to send to hell soon. After all, hell has no fury like a pissed off Romanov.

Chapter 6

It had been a few days since the shooting at the Romanov estate. Stepan was still a little clueless to who was behind it all. He and Alexei did however have an idea on who could help them figure it out. They had been watching him for the last few days. He hadn't led them to the person in charge, but he had shown them that he couldn't be trusted. It was because of that and his participation in their mother's death that he would die.

"He just pulled up." Alexei stated as he watched their prey from the shadows inside the dark house.

It was passed midnight in Moscow and it was pitch black out on the streets. The only light out was the moonlight shining bright in the sky. After midnight was when Moscow really came to life. The night life there was a sight to see and an experience like no other. They could tell their prey had just enjoyed himself out on the town.

"He's walking right into his death and he has no idea." Alexei thought with a sinister grin spread across his face.

The front door to the house opened up with a loud bang from it hitting the wall. The prey stumbled in with a female companion on his arm.

"Ya budu trakhat' tebya tak sil'no, chto ty ne smozhesh' pochuvstvovat' svoi nogi zavtra." (I'm going to fuck you so much you won't be able to feel your legs tomorrow.)

"Oh baby, don't be a tease." The woman moaned as he sucked on her neck. He used his foot to close the door behind them.

"Tsk... tsk Anton, lying to a woman isn't a good idea. They tend to be very scornful when lied to. How are you going to keep your word if you're dead?" Alexei questioned from the corner of the room.

Anton's eyes widened at the sound of his voice. He sobered up real quick after that. The woman he was with was scared out of her mind. She was about to scream, but stopped when she felt a cold piece of steel on her back.

"I wouldn't do that if I were you. Get out and never speak of this night. If I find out that you opened your mouth, I'll cut your tongue out so that you'll never speak again. Is that understood?" Stepan spoke from behind them.

The woman feverishly nodded her head. "Yes, I understand." She spoke in Russian.

Stepan opened the door and let her out. As soon as she crossed the threshold she took off running. She had no clue who those men were and she didn't want to know. She barely knew who Anton was. They had met a few hours ago at a bar.

Once Anton heard the door close and lock; he knew his life was over. He had chosen the wrong side and now he was going to pay for it.

"Boss, prosti..." (Boss, I'm sorry...) He started to beg for his life.

"Sokhrani svoyu lozh' dlya d'yavola. Oni plokho s nami." (Save your lies for the devil. They're no good with us.) Alexei stated finally letting himself be seen.

"I had to do it." Anton cried while speaking in English.

"You had to betray us? You had to help plot on the lives of my daughters?" Stepan shouted. He shot Anton in both his knee caps.

"Ahhhhhh! Please, I'm sorry! I needed the money to help my sick mother!" Anton screamed out from the pain that shot through him.

Alexei and Stepan looked at each other and laughed. "Do you hear this, brother? He betrayed our trust for his sick mother. Do I not pay our men enough money for them and their families to live comfortably?" Stepan questioned.

Alexei stepped closer to Anton and bent down. "You pay them very well. That is why we never had this problem before. That is also how I know that our friend Anton here is lying to us." He grabbed Anton's left knee and squeezed it tight.

"Ahhhhhhhh! Okay... okay! I'll tell you everything that you need to know. Please just stop."

"Ty verish' yemu, brat?" (Do you believe him, brother?)

Stepan scoffed. "Net, no davayte poslushayem, chto on skazhet." (No, but let's hear what he has to say anyway.) He replied.

"Let's hear it, podonok." (scumbag)

"I didn't know things were going to turn out like this. I had no choice, but to do as he asked. He threatened to..." Anton's words were cut short when gunfire erupted in the house.

Stepan and Alexei took cover. The shots were coming from outside. They both took aim at the window.

Anton tried to drag his body behind the couch, but ended up taking a shot to the back. "Ahhhhhhhh, shit! Pomogi mne!" (Help me!)

Before either of them could reach for Anton another round of shots rang out. Two of them landed in the back of his head. Once Anton was dead the gunfire stopped.

"They were here for him." Alexei said.

"I guess they knew we would figure out he was a traitor."

"I guess so, but he was our only lead so far to who was behind this shit." He spat.

"That just means we have to do things the old fashioned way. We might ruffle a few feathers, but I'm okay with that. What about you, brother?" Stepan asked as he looked over at him.

"Let's go shake shit up in the underworld." Alexei stated.

They headed for the door and walked out just as quietly as they walked in. Things were about to get a lot more bloody in Russia.

~~~~~~~~~~~~~~~~~~~~~~~~~~~~~~~

All the way across the globe in Chicago Will was taking care of some business of his own. He sat in the meeting he had Zel set up a few days ago. He was anxious to get this over with so that he could get back home to his girls.

"I had you all gathered here today for a few very important reasons. First on the list; business has been going well and you all should be very happy about that. You know that when business does well, your pockets get fatter." He chuckled causing all the men in the warehouse that they stood in to laugh as well.

"I like to show my appreciation for all the hard work y'all been putting in. So, expect to receive a few extra thousand with your pay today." Will told them. He watched as they all cheered.

"That's what I'm talking about, boss man!" One guy shouted out excited.

"Okay, calm down there is still another matter I want to discuss with you." He placed his hands in his slacks' pockets. He glanced around the room. The men immediately started to get quiet.

"It was recently brought to my attention that there has been unwanted shit being moved on my territory. The part that shocked me the most was that it wasn't brought to my attention by the person who should have been the one to tell me. So, I'm going to just ask a simple question and give them a chance to come clean. Do any of you have something to tell me?" He questioned.

Zel stood a few feet behind him with his gun in his hand. He had his hands rested on front of him with his eyes trained on all of the men. It was his job to be Will's other set of eyes.

"I'm only going to ask that question once." Will stated when no one spoke up.

A few of the guys looked around. One guy in particular looked more nervous than the rest. He took a deep breath and stepped forward.

"I got something to say, boss." He said in a shaky voice. He along with everyone else in the warehouse knew Will's reputation. His fear was very justified.

"I'm listening, Calvin." Will nodded for him to continue.

"Some weeks back I noticed that the Hell Raisers were moving some of their product on our blocks." He stated. The Hell Raisers was a motorcycle club that dealt in all types of illegal things. Will had never had a problem with them since he brought his business to Chicago. He now wondered if that was because they had been plotting the whole time.

"Did you take that information to your capo?" Will asked him.

Calvin nodded. "Yeah and I was told that it would be brought to your attention and handled. After that I left the situation alone. I didn't say anything else about it because I didn't know what y'all may have had planned for them." He shrugged.

Will glanced over at Zel. "Who is his capo?" He asked even though he already knew the answer to his question.

Zel nodded towards one of the guys that stood off in the back. He looked nervous with sweat dripping from his forehead. "His capo is James."

Will looked back at James and nodded for him to come forward. "Step to the front James."

James swallowed hard as he made his way up front. "Yeah, boss?"

"Is what Calvin just told me correct?"

James looked over at Calvin. He thought about lying, but he had a feeling that they already knew the truth. He didn't want to make the situation worse by lying about knowing what was going on.

"Yes, it's true."

Will scoffed. "Why the hell didn't you open up your fucking mouth and let me know what was going on?"

James started fidgeting and Will gave Zel a look. "I... I had planned on bringing it to your attention. I got sidetracked with working and..."

"You got sidetracked? Is that the excuse you're going to use?"

"It's not an excuse, boss. I..."

"So, you're telling me that you noticed muthafuckas moving in on my territory and you didn't say shit because you forgot?"

James didn't know if he should speak or not so he didn't say anything. He just nodded his head. The sweat that seeped from his forehead dripped down into his eyes. He wiped at his eyes and looked at Will.

"I find that hard to believe, James. Are you sure that's what really happened or did you allow your sister's man who's in the Hell Raisers to move his shit on my territory?"

James eyes widened at his words. He had thought he hid the fact his sister's boyfriend was in the Hell Raisers. He had been letting him and his boys move their drugs and guns on Will's territory for a minute now.

"I... I..."

"You fucked up, that's what you did."

"Boss, let me explain..."

"There's no need for you to explain anything, James. By letting them move that shit on my streets you've all been stealing from me. That's okay though..." Will nodded his head towards Zel.

Zel lifted his gun and shot James directly between the eyes. The rest of the men took a step back and stared at his dead body.

"Let this be a lesson to you all. If you value your life and the lives of your family; don't fuck with my money." Will spat and started towards the door. He stopped when he got halfway there and slightly turned to face them.

"Oh yeah, stay on alert and prepare yourself for war if need be. The Hell Raisers are going to pay for trespassing and I doubt they're going to be happy about it." He stated before walking out the door.

Zel came out a few minutes later. "I called the cleanup crew. They should be here soon." He said.

"Good; I need that handled and everyone back to business asap."

"What are we going to do about the Hell Raisers?" Zel asked.

Will rubbed his chin. "I got somebody in mind that could help me out with that."

"Well, let me know if you need me, boss."

"Of course." They slapped hands.

"You about to head back home?"

Will nodded. "Yeah, I want to spend some time with my girls. Aye, how about you bring Zela by the house sometime this weekend. Naya would love somebody her age to play with."

"You got it; your Goddaughter claim she doesn't see you enough anyway."

Will chuckled. "Tell her that I'll take her to the movies or something with Naya."

"I'm sure she'll love that. This messy shit with her mom is starting to bother her." Zel said as he dragged his hand down his face.

"Y'all are still going through the custody battle?"

"Man yeah and she got me ready to snap her fucking neck too. She got those people thinking that I don't take care of my daughter."

They both looked at each other with their faces twisted up. "That's bullshit and she knows it. Anybody that knows you know that you do everything for your little girl." Will said.

"Exactly, but she trying to go for full custody so that she could get more money. I think she got her sisters and her auntie in her head telling her that shit."

"All this stupid shit because you don't want her no good ass anymore."

"Yeah, you'll think I was the one who was fucking around on her and not the other way around. I swear if she wasn't Zela's mama her ass would be dead right now." Zel spat with his face scrunched up.

"I feel you, man. You know if you need me for anything I'm here for you." Will told him.

Zel smiled and nodded. "I know and you've done enough already. That lawyer you helped me get is a beast."

"Glad to hear he's doing his job. Let me know if that changes. I'll catch you later; I'm about to get out of here." They slapped hands again and embraced in a brotherly hug.

Zel watched as Will jumped in his car and pulled off. He turned around at the same time that the cleanup crew pulled up. He was glad because he also wanted to get home to his little girl.

~~~~~~~~~~~~~~~~~~~~~~~~~

Will strolled inside the house and locked the door behind him. He could hear music playing and wondered where it was coming from. The farther he got in the house the louder the music became. He followed the sound of the music to the kitchen. When he made it to the entrance of the kitchen he stopped in his tracks. He stood there and smiled at the sight before him.

Cori sat on a bar stool at the counter. She watched with a happy facial expression as Sarah and Naya song along to the music while cooking. Naya had the new microphone that Will had bought her the other day in her hand. She wasn't that great of a singer, but she was hitting the notes like she was. Cori was happy to see her sister smiling and laughing.

"Feelings! So deep in my feelings!" Naya sung at the top of her lungs.

"Hold up a minute! What little knuckle head little boy got you in your feelings? I need to have a little talk with him about that." Will said cutting her off.

"Will; You're home!" Naya screamed as she ran over to him.

He scooped her up in his arms. "You're not slick trying to distract me. Who is the little boy I got to beat up... I mean talk to?"

Naya, Cori, and Sarah all laughed at him. "There isn't any boy. It was a song I was singing."

"Yeah okay, it better not be a boy." He told her.

She giggled at his words. "My daddy said that I can't think about boys until I get a good education and my skin get wrinkle. I think that means when I get old."

Will glanced over at Cori. The smile on her face warmed his heart. Over six months ago he thought that he would never see that smile again. Now when he do see it, he cherish that moment.

"What are you ladies in here cooking up?" He walked over to Cori and gave her a kiss.

"Sarah is making beef bourguignon. It's like a beef stew over pasta. It's very good and tasty." Cori replied.

"It sounds good too. So, what have y'all been up to today?"

"Well, we got a workout in..." Cori started, but was interrupted by Naya.

"I thought I was going to die. It was too much and my little legs kept getting tired." Naya said being dramatic.

Cori chuckled. "I told you that you didn't have to everything that I did."

"I know, but I wanted to be like you."

"Awww princess, I don't want you to be like me."

Naya frowned at her words. "Why?"

"Because I want you to be better than me."

"What if I want to be just like you?" She tilted her head to the side.

"I think that with how smart, strong, and beautiful you are that even if you do try to be just like me, you'll always exceed that. As a matter of fact, I want to be like you when I grow up." Cori started tickling her.

Will placed Naya down on her feet. "I'm going to go change out of this suit and put on something more comfortable."

"Okay, I'm going to finish helping Sarah cook. We made marlenka for dessert." Naya smiled up at him.

"What is marlenka?"

"It's a layered cake with honey and condensed milk as its main ingredients. It's very good." Sarah replied.

"I can't wait to try it. I'll be back down in a minute, ladies." Will said and then left out the kitchen.

Cori was about to excuse herself, but her phone ringing stopped her from moving. She glanced at the screen and saw that it was Alyona calling. She and Naya had gone over to her house to visit her and Monica the other day.

"Hello?"

"Hey cousin, how are you?" Alyona asked.

"I'm doing okay, what about you and Monica?"

"We're doing good, but every time I think about grandma I get sad."

"Yeah, me too. My dad called this morning to let me know that funeral arrangements had been made. We'll be leaving in a few days and going back to Russia." Cori told her.

"My mom called and told me too. This is going to be really hard. Did I tell you that Sasha called me?"

Cori rolled her eyes. "No, what did she want? I still have a few words for her."

"She asked if she could come out here and visit after grandma's funeral. She said that she need a new scenery for a while." Alyona replied.

"What did you tell her?"

There was a short pause. "I told her that it was okay. She just wants to be around her cousins right now."

"Cousins?"

"Yes Cori, you and Sasha need to put your differences aside. Our family is going through a difficult time right now. We need to come together and be there for one another."

"Uh, I did tell you what she told Naya, right?"

"Yes, you did and I agree you should pop her in the mouth for that. After that though you two should work on your relationship as cousins." Alyona said causing Cori to laugh.

"I'll think about it."

Cori's attention was drawn to Will when he walked back in the kitchen. He had on a pair of dark gray sweatpants and a light gray sleeveless t-shirt. He looked sexy without even trying.

"Alyona let me call you back. I have to handle something real quick."

"Okay and think about what I said."

"Yeah, whatever you say, cousin. Bye now." She hung up the phone before Alyona could respond.

Cori jumped up off the bar stool and walked up to Will. She grabbed him by the hand and led him back out of the kitchen.

"What's wrong, baby?" He asked as he let her lead him all the way back upstairs to their bedroom.

Cori didn't say a word as she walked over to his closet and grabbed him a pair of black sweatpants. She reached them out to him for him to take.

"What am I supposed to do with these?"

"Put them on, we have guest in the house now. You can't be walking around in that." She waved her hands at the sweatpants he had on.

Will looked down and then looked back at her. "What's wrong with what I got on?"

She rolled her eyes and then folded her arms across her chest. "Well, for starters you're wearing slut pants."

Will stared at her for a moment and then laughed. "Baby, these are just sweatpants."

"No, everyone knows that on a man those are slut pants. Now any other time I wouldn't mind seeing them on you, but since I can't take you down whenever I want you can't wear those. They are a tease." She stated.

He rubbed his chin. "So, you're saying that I'm being a tease right now?"

"Yes and it's not right." She eyed the big long print that's going down his thigh.

Will smirked as he watched her watching his dick. "All you have to do is pull me aside and let me know you need a quick pick me up."

Cori walked up to him and pressed the black sweatpants into his chest. "I need you to put these on. Thank you very much Mr. Cooper." She said and then walked out the bedroom.

"You're being real bossy right now Ms. Romanov!" He yelled after her.

"That's because I'm a boss, remember?"

Will chuckled as he looked at the sweatpants. "Damn I love that woman." He said before he removed the gray sweatpants to put on the black ones.

Cori smiled to herself as she headed back downstairs. "I love that man." She mumbled.

"Cori and Will it's time to eat!" Naya yelled up the stairs.

"Oh there you are." She said when she saw her sister.

"He's going to be down in a minute." Cori told her.

"Okay, come on." Naya grabbed her hand.

"I'm coming..."

"Can we call daddy after dinner?" Naya asked her as they made their way into the kitchen.

"Yes, we can call him. Do you miss daddy?"

Naya nodded. "Yes, I miss him a lot."

Cori smiled down at her. "I'm sure he misses you too."

"He's working right now?"

She nodded. "Yes."

"Okay."

"Okay ladies, let's eat." Will said when he stepped into the kitchen. He kissed Cori on the cheek as he walked pass to help Sarah set the table.

Cori grinned when she noticed he was wearing the black sweatpants. "I love a man that listens." She thought.

"Come on Cori, let's eat!" Naya ran over to the table.

Cori followed behind her with a smile on her face. She could get used to having family dinner with them.

Chapter 7

Stepan glanced at the picture of his two girls on his phone. The smiles on their faces made him feel good about what he was about to do. He kissed the screen then placed the phone back in his pocket. Stepan then looked over at his brother who stood beside him.

"Are you ready, brother?"

"I've been ready, brother." Alexei replied with a stone facial expression.

They headed inside of the run down building. It used to be an old slaughter house. The stench of the old dried up blood that was embedded in the floors and walls still engulfed the building.

"Gentlemen, to what do we owe this visit to?" A man that stood in the center of the room asked. He stood in front of a group of ten men. He wanted to let everyone in the place know that he was in charge.

The amount of men didn't scare or faze Stepan or Alexei. They actually looked at each other and smirked. They could smell the men's fear a mile away.

"Emiliano, I'm sure by now you've heard about the attack on my home." Stepan said to the man who spoke.

"Yes... yes, I heard about that. You don't think I had anything to do with it do you?" Emiliano gave him a raised eyebrow expression.

That caused a grin to spread across Stepan's face. "Do you honestly think I would be standing here speaking to you if I thought for a second you had anything to do with the attack?"

"Well, I thought..."

"You know our reputation, Emiliano. You know that if we suspected that you had anything to do with it, you, your men, and your families would all be dead already. Do not insult us with that dumb question again." Alexei stated with an emotionless facial expression.

Emiliano and all his men swallowed hard at his words. "Wh... what did you call this meeting with me for?" He asked. All the confidence he had before they arrived was now gone. He was talking tough to his men just ten minutes ago about how funny he thought it was that someone attacked the Romanovs on their own property. Saying that they must have gotten weak over the last few years. Now, his whole attitude changed. Now that he was standing a few feet away from Alexei and Stepan, he knew his assumption had been false.

"We heard around that you were moving into a new business venture. Is that true?" Stepan questioned.

"Yes, you can never have too many incomes right?" He released a nervous chuckle.

"No, you can't... My problem with that new business venture of yours is that it goes against the peace agreement we set in place."

The frown on Emiliano's face almost made Alexei and Stepan laugh. He had thought that they wouldn't find out about it.

"I don't understand how me wanting to get into the real estate market would go against the agreement."

Alexei took a few steps towards him. His reflex caused him to take a step backwards.

"Did you honestly think that we wouldn't find out about you working with Felipe Gomez?"

The sweat beads that formed on Emiliano's forehead glistened. He didn't know if he should try to wipe it away or not. He didn't want to let his men know that he's close to pissing on himself.

"I don't see how me working with Felipe is a problem." He said in a shaky voice.

Alexei glance over his shoulder at his brother. "Brother, do you see how he tries to play us like we're stupid?"

Stepan took a step beside his brother. He glanced behind Emiliano at his men. He smiled at them before he placed his attention back on Emiliano.

"Yes, I see how stupid he is and how he thinks we're just as stupid as him."

"No, I would never..."

"Emiliano, do you think we don't know what type of business Felipe does?" Stepan questioned.

"He... he... he does business in..."

"Sex trafficking... that's the only business he's ever dealt in. Stealing and selling women and little girls!" Stepan snapped as he snatched him up by his collar. The memory of Naya in that warehouse were Carlos Vargas had planned to have her raped and sold after killing her biological parents flashed in his mind. She was now his little girl and the thought of anyone trying to harm her sent him into a rage. If Felipe attacked the Romanovs to avenge what happened to his business partner Vargas then he would suffer the same consequences as him; death.

Alexei looked at Emiliano's men. Neither of them made a move to step in and help their boss.

"Felipe knew that he could never step foot on Russian soil with that type of business. It had been banned in the underworld here. That's why he decided to go into business with you. He knew that you were the only one stupid enough to do it. Dumb enough to risk his life and the lives of his men for a few extra bucks."

"What we want to know from you is where Felipe is hiding?" Alexei asked with his eyes still on the ten men.

"He's been held up at one of my properties out in Voronezh. He said something about not wanting anyone to know that he was in Russia." Emiliano said without hesitation. He was scared and rather Felipe deal with the Romanovs than him.

Stepan released his collar then tapped him on the cheek. "Telling us that was the smartest thing you've done since we stepped through that door."

"I'll tell you everything you need to know."

Alexei chuckled. "I bet you will."

Emiliano told them exactly where they could find Felipe. Once he gave them all the information they asked for he released a sigh of relief when he saw them turn to leave.

Alexei and Stepan got to the door and stopped. They glanced at each other before they turned back around to face the men.

"One more thing, Emiliano." Stepan stated with a stern tone.

"What do you need? Ask me anything and I will tell you or make it happen." Emiliano said nervous and afraid of saying the wrong thing.

"Anything?" Alexei questioned.

"Yes... yes."

"Well, because you were going to participate in stealing, raping, and selling women and little girls we think it's best if you kill yourself."

Emiliano waited for them to laugh or say that it was a joke. When they just stood there staring at him he swallowed hard.

"Wh... what?"

"He said you should kill yourself." Stepan told him.

"I... I... I..."

They laughed at his stuttering. "We're joking with you, Emiliano." Alexei said with a chuckle.

Emiliano wiped the sweat from his face on to his pants. He released a weak and nervous laugh along with his men.

"Oh, you got me."

"Yes, we wouldn't ask you to kill yourself." Stepan stated.

"Of course not. We'll do it ourselves." Alexei said with his face now emotionless.

"Wait, what? I..."

Before he or his men could react, Alexei and Stepan pulled out a scorpion VZ61 sub machine gun. They let the bullets rip through all eleven men. Emiliano last thought before he took his last breath was the regret of going against a Romanov.

Once they were satisfied that everyone was dead they walked out the building. After getting in their car and driving away Alexei pressed a button on a small remote. Within seconds the entire building exploded.

"That was a productive visit." Stepan said.

"Yes, it was brother. Should we prepare for a trip to Voronezh?"

"Yes, we need to get to Felipe before he gets word that Emiliano is dead. We don't want him to know that we're on to him before we get to him."

"I still can't believe he thought it was wise to go against us."

Stepan nodded. "We've come across a lot of stupid men over the years. This is nothing different."

They both nodded in agreement. They had been in business for many years and during that time there had been enough stupid men and even women to test them.

Stepan was glad that they were getting things done quickly. Once they got rid of Felipe things could go back to normal. He couldn't wait to get his little princess back home where she belonged. They still had to bury their mother in a few days also. After everything was said and done Stepan and Alexei planned to make sure anyone who ever thought of going against them would think twice about it.

~~~~~~~~~~~~~~~~~~~~~~~~

Felipe Gomez stood on the balcony and puffed on his Cuban cigar. A smile graced his face when he thought about all the money he was going to make in Russia. After the death of his old business partner Carlos Vargas, business had slowed down tremendously for him. That meant his money also slowed down as well. He owed that to Stepan, Alexei, and Cori Romanov. The thought of the name Romanov put a bad taste in his mouth. Felipe despised the amount power and money the Romanovs had. He was jealous and had no problems with showing it. He waited a long time to get back at them. Now was his chance and he couldn't be more excited about it.

"I can't wait to see their faces when they realize how much money I make in their backyard." He chuckled.

Two hands started to rub on his chest from behind. "Papi, come get in the Jacuzzi tub with me." A kiss was placed on his bare back.

Felipe stood on the balcony butt naked. That gave his guest easy access to his manhood. He glanced down as he watched her manicured nails and hands roam from his chest to his dick.

"I see you are a greedy one." He moan out when she started stroking him.

"Yes papi, I can't get enough of you. I want you to fuck me in the Jacuzzi." She licked his back and then lightly bite down on it.

That turned him on. He tossed his cigar off the balcony and turned towards her. He smiled at the sight of her naked body. He knew most of her body was fake, but it was still a nice sight to see.

Felipe grabbed her and pulled her close to him. His hand slowly moved down to her ass and gripped it hard.

"You love having me buried deep inside you, huh?" He whispered in her ear.

"Yes."

"Well, let me not be a bad host then. Lead the way, my love." He waved towards the Jacuzzi that sat over in the corner of the room.

Felipe watched her ass as she strutted to the Jacuzzi. She climbed inside and then waved her fingers for him to come join her. He slipped inside and leaned back against the edge.

"Why don't you come over here and ride me?"

She smirked. "I thought you'll never ask."

He grinned as she made her way to him. He was hard and ready for her too. Right when she was about to climb on top of him the bedroom door burst open.

"Boss!" The head of his security team shouted when they ran inside.

"What the hell are you doing? I told you that I didn't want to be disturbed!" Felipe yelled.

"Yes, but boss they killed them all."

"Who killed all of who?"

"The Ghost and the Grim Reaper! They killed..." Before he could finish his statement a bullet ripped through the back of his head and went flying through his forehead.

"What the fuck?" Felipe shouted out in shock. The two faces he saw next had him pissing on himself in the Jacuzzi.

"Ah, Felipe it's been a minute hasn't it?" Stepan asked with a deadly smirk on his face.

"What is the meaning of this?" Felipe questioned as if he didn't know anything.

"You know exactly why we're here. Now get out of the Jacuzzi." Alexei spat as he threw a towel at him.

The woman looked between all three men. She didn't think that Stepan or Alexei had paid her any attention. She eased over to the side of Jacuzzi where Felipe had two guns at. She glanced at the men one last time before she went for them. When she picked up the two guns and turned around to aim at Alexei and Stepan, she was met with two bullets to her skull from each of their gun. Her brain matter and blood splashed all over Felipe's face. He fought hard not to scream out. He refuse to let them see how terrified he was.

"Put that towel on and get out now!" Stepan yelled.

Felipe did as he was told. He then stood in front of them with the towel wrapped around his waist.

"So, you found out the truth, huh?" Felipe asked with fake confidence.

"Did you ever think that we wouldn't?" Alexei questioned with scowl on his face.

"Oh yes, I figured that you would find out eventually; just not this soon."

Stepan stepped towards him. "You do realize that you fucked up when you fucked with my family, right?"

Felipe gave him a look he couldn't read. "What are...?"

Alexei cut him off with a swift and quick hit to the jaw with his gun. Felipe hit the floor hard like a sack of potatoes.

"We could interrogate him later while we torture him. We need to get out of here. The police are on the way."

Stepan glanced at him. "How did the police know to come here?"

"I had one of our men call someone on our payroll. They found a group of women and children down in the basement." He replied.

Stepan looked down at an unconscious Felipe. He kicked him in the face. "Fucking scumbag asshole! Get someone in here to grab him. I can't fucking wait to torture the son of a bitch." He spat before he placed his gun back in the waist of his pants.

"You and me both, brother."

Alexei called in for some of his men to collect Felipe. Afterwards he and Stepan left out the same way they came in. They stepped around all the dead bodies of Felipe's men that stood guard.

"It's almost over, brother." Stepan said to Alexei once they were in the car.

"We have to send a good message for anybody stupid enough to pull what he did."

"We will; that I can promise you."

"Now the real question is should we kill him right away after a little torture or should we prolong it until after the funeral?" Alexei asked as he looked over at him.

"Now that I think about it I realized we've been a little selfish. Cori had wanted to be present when we found the person who want her and Naya dead."

"Also the person who killed the woman who raised her. Mama was her only living grandparent and now she's gone."

Stepan nodded. "I think we should make him suffer and prolong his torture then kill him right before the funeral. That way Cori would be back in town for the funeral and could have a little fun herself."

"That sounds good to me." Alexei agreed.

Both men minds were overrun with thoughts on different ways to make Felipe regret the day he ever crossed a Romanov.

Chapter 8

Back in Chicago Will and Cori had some important business to handle. They left Naya in the care of her nanny Sarah. They also had Zel at the house with his little girl Zela. It served two purposes for the night. It gave Naya someone she could play with that was her age. Also, with Zel being there they had somebody to look after all of them without them feeling over guarded. Even though they had a top notch security system installed; it added another layer of security for Naya and Sarah.

"So, how do you want to do this?" Cori asked Will as she looked over at him. For some reason the all black attire that he sported turned her on. She already knew that her man was sexy, but when he had on his war attire, as she liked to call it; it did something to her.

They were seated in a car parked up the street from the Hell Raisers headquarters. Will enlisted his woman to help him out with his problem or so he liked to think. In reality Cori enlisted herself to help him out. She knew together they could get rid of his problem without a hitch. It would be her first job since she got out of the hospital months ago from the explosion. In her eyes nothing was better than getting her feet wet with her man by her side. Cori had a whole new outlook on life now and she had Will to thank for it.

Will's eyes roamed from her beautiful face down her sexy body. Once they landed on her exposed thigh, he took his hand and rubbed on it.

"My original plan was to go in and kill them all. Now that you're here that won't work." He said.

"Why is that Mr. Cooper?" She gave him a small smile.

"Well, for starters my mind would be on how you look in this dress. I won't be able to focus on killing anyone." He licked his bottom lip as if he could taste her on his mouth.

"I think my look for the night would fit perfect for the occasion."

He raised an eyebrow at her. "How you figure that, Ms. Romanov?"

"Well, I did my research on the Hell Raisers."

"What did you find out?"

"I found out that they have their hands in a lot of things. Most of their business comes from stealing from other people; guns, drugs, and even women. Because of that they have a lot of enemies as well. Their leader name is Vinny Flores. He's the boyfriend of your deceased worker James' sister. They don't have any kids together. She's a part of the Hell Raisers as well. Word is that she was the one who convinced James to help them set up on your territory." Cori told him.

"How do you know all of this?"

Cori smirked at him. She had one of her knives in her hand. She played with it as she answered his question.

"I had a little chat with Vinny's second in command Teddy. He was very informative and happy to tell me everything I wanted to know."

"Oh really?" It was Will's turn to smirk at her.

"Yup, me threatening to cut off his balls and stuff them down his throat was just a bit of encouragement for him." She stated.

His laughter surrounded the entire car. He couldn't stop thinking to himself how much he loved his woman.

"Okay, so where is he now?" Will asked.

"Oh, he's dead now. After I got the information I wanted I helped reunite him with his creator."

"You are a piece of work, woman."

Cori grinned. "I know and that's probably why you love me so much. Anyway, back to why I'm wearing this outfit. Teddy... rest his soul; told me that they have women come to their spot to party with them all the time. This is how they like the women to dress; trashy. So, I'm going to go in there and tell them that Teddy invited me and I'm waiting for him to arrive. Then I'll give you the signal and you'll use your big gun..." She started rubbing on his thigh.

"Oops, not that one sorry. You'll use your rifle and take out some from the roof while I handle the rest from the ground. The roof is made of glass so it'll be easy to see once you get up there."

Will chuckled. "You're a fucking tease, baby."

"I know and I enjoy it because I know you're going to punish my body for it later."

"As long as you know, beautiful."

"Here are the ear pieces that we'll use to communicate. I'll wait until you are in position before I head in."

He grabbed the back of her neck and pulled her face towards his. His lips crashed into hers before she welcomed his tongue into her mouth. They kissed for a few minutes before he pulled away.

"Be safe; I love you."

"You be safe too, baby. I love you." She said and pecked him on the lips once more before he got out the car.

Cori watched as he grabbed his gun out of the trunk. She kept her eyes on him as he headed towards the back of the warehouse slash Hell Raisers headquarters.

"Can you hear me?" Will asked.

"Yes, I can hear you perfectly."

"Good, give it five minutes then head to the front door."

"Okay."

She waited five minutes like he requested and then climbed out of the car. "Are you set up?"

"Yeah and you were right about the women. They're barely dressed in there."

She rolled her eyes. "I bet you are enjoying the view, huh?"

"Nope, I only got eyes for you, beautiful."

"Good save, Mr. Cooper."

"There are about fifteen of the crew members in there. The rest are women and it's about nine of them." Will informed her.

"From the way Teddy was talking they might be crew as well. We'll find out once I get inside."

Cori walked up to the door and took a quick glance around her. She was surprised that they didn't have any of their men standing guard. That would be one of their biggest mistakes, especially knowing they got a lot of enemies. That in itself told her how cocky they were. As if they were too good to be touched. She smiled at that thought.

Cori rubbed her hands down the short black dress she had on. It showed off her smooth caramel thighs and legs. She pushed her cleavage up a little and put a big smile on her face before knocking hard on the door.

The door swung open and a big ugly hairy man answered the door. He had a bald shaven head, a long beard, but his chest that was exposed by the leather vest he wore was covered in hair. Cori almost wrinkled her nose up at him, but she had to stay in character.

"How can I help you sexy mama?" He asked as he looked over her body.

She fought hard to keep herself from reacting. "Baby, don't do it. Just follow the plan." Will said into her ear. He knew she was seconds away from slitting the guy's throat. She hated for a guy that wasn't him to call her sexy or give her a pet name.

"I was told by Teddy to come here and wait for him. He said that he'll be arriving shortly and I could wait inside." Cori told the hairy guy.

He grinned at her. "Of course, come right on in."

"Thank you."

When she walked inside she instantly glanced around and made herself familiar with how many people were present and where they were. She felt a hand on her lower back and had to stop herself from reacting violently.

"Would you like a drink while you wait? I'll show you to the bar."

She discreetly stepped out of his reach. "Yes, I would love a drink."

"Well, let's get you a drink then sexy mama."

He lead her over to their bar station. After he mixed her up a drink he dropped a pill in it. He used a small red straw to stir it up.

"He spiked your drink. He's my first target." Will sneered into her ear.

Cori smiled as the guy handed her the drink. She watched him look her over again from her legs up to her breast.

"So, how did you meet Teddy?"

"I honestly can't remember all the details. I just remember the sex that's it." She told him.

He smirked. "You're a wild girl, huh?"

"I've been told that a time or two." She flirted.

Cori could hear Will chuckle. She knew he couldn't wait to blow this guy's head off.

"You know we in the Hell Raisers like to share. We're not a stingy group at all."

"Oh really?"

"Yeah, there's not any fun if the boys can't have any." He chortled.

"As soon as I get eyes on Vinny, I'm taking him out." Will said.

"That wasn't in the plans." Cori giggled. The guy thought she was speaking to him.

"Well, you know plans change, sexy mama."

"I don't give a damn. He's dead as soon as Vinny makes his presence known so be ready." Will stated.

"I'm always ready for a little fun." She replied.

The guy rubbed his hands together and grinned. "That's what I like to hear."

"I see the party is in full effect! Where is Teddy at? He's the only one missing tonight." Vinny said as he and his girl walked in.

"He's on his way according to this sexy mama right here." The guy next to Cori said.

Vinny glanced at Cori and eyed her body. "Well, who are you, beautiful?"

"Beautiful?" His girlfriend questioned and then glared at Cori.

Vinny chuckled. "Chill out Risha, she's our guest. Who knows, she might be joining us in our bed tonight."

Risha walked up to Cori. "You don't look all that good to me. Maybe when the crew is done having their fun with you then I'll kill you. Just like I do all the bitches who get the pleasure of fucking my man." She threatened.

"She's your first target, ain't she?" Will questioned.

"Yup." Cori replied.

Risha frowned while her man and the hairy guy laughed. "Yup, what? Where did Teddy find this crazy bitch?" She asked with a chortle.

Cori stepped closer to her. "He found me in his house at night after he stumbled in a little drunk. I think he had just come from one of these types of parties. Anyway, it was all before I tortured then killed him."

The laughter stopped after she finished her sentence. Vinny looked more confused than anyone. He couldn't tell from her facial expression if she was serious or joking.

"What type of joke is that?" The hairy guy asked with a laugh.

Cori kept her eyes on Risha. "It wasn't a joke. He's dead and you all will be joining him soon. Right, babe?"

"Who are you talking...?" Vinny was cut off when the guy standing next to Cori entire head split open.

"What the fuck?" Vinny eyes widened at the sight of his man on the ground dead.

Risha didn't have much time to react due to the knife sticking out of her mouth. She tried to scream and Cori threw the knife at her silencing her forever. Her body dropped to the floor along with a few others that Will took out from the roof.

Cori pulled out a small hand gun and aimed towards Vinny. Before she could pull the trigger his chest was riddled with bullets.

"Hey!"

"Sorry baby, you already took out the second in command. The leader was mine." Will chuckled.

She shot a guy that was running towards her in the head. That stopped him dead in his tracks; all pun intended. Within ten minutes Will and Cori had killed everyone inside. She made sure they were all dead excluding three women who weren't apart of the crew. She let them go and wasn't worried about them telling. They were too scared to ever speak of that night again.

"Are you ready, baby?" Will asked her.

Cori glanced around before heading for the door. "Yeah, I'll see you soon."

A grin spread across her face. "Ah, it feels good to be back." She said with a chuckle.

Once they both made it back to the car they pulled off. Will wanted the bodies to be found so a message could be given to anyone else that thought about disrespecting him or his business. They headed straight to the condo that Cori still owned for situations like this. Will didn't want them to bring any of the bad energy from a job to leak into their home. That's where they would raise their children some day and he wanted it to be pure. Cori agreed with him so they kept the condo.

~~~~~~~~~~~~~~~~~~~~~~~~~~~~~~~~~~

At the house Zel and Sarah was trying to get the girls to go down for bed. They were both having a hard time with it. It was most likely his fault since he let them eat ice cream with cookies and gummy bears in it. They were having a sugar rush like no other.

"Okay, it's bedtime princesses." Sarah told them for the second time that night.

"We wanted to wait up for Cori and Will." Naya said while bouncing on her knees on the bed.

"Yes, we have to stay up and tell them good night. We don't want to be rude." Zela told her.

"Zela, you know it's pass your bedtime. It's pass yours too, Naya." Zel said as he stood in the doorway.

"Aww daddy, we're not even sleepy." Zela pouted.

Zel decided to try a different route. "Do y'all think Cori or Will is going to be happy with y'all not listening to Sarah?"

The girls looked at each other and then back at him. They shook their head. "No." They replied.

"Well, get under the comforter and try to go to sleep."

Zel stepped out into the hallway when he heard the footsteps. He already knew who it was before he saw their faces.

"They've been waiting for y'all." He told Cori and Will.

Cori smiled as she rushed into the bedroom that they turned into Naya's room.

"Cori!" They girls shouted when they saw her.

Zel shook his head. "How did they do?" Will asked when he made it beside him.

"They did good until it was time to go to bed. They told me that they're best friends now."

Will chuckled. "That was the goal."

"Yeah..." Zel smiled as he looked at his baby girl talking and giggling with Cori and Naya. It's been a minute since he saw her smile like that.

"Thanks man, she needed this night."

"You don't need to thank me. You know I'm going to always have my Goddaughter's best interest at heart." Will told him.

"How did things go tonight?" Zel questioned.

"We'll talk about it tomorrow. We have to head back to Russia for the funeral in a few days. I'll be taking a team of our best men with me. Can you get them together for me?"

"Yeah, I got you."

"Thanks man, grab one of the guest rooms and get some sleep. Cori and I will take the night shift with the girls. I'm hoping after a few bedtime stories they'll pass out." Will said as he patted him on the shoulder before he headed in the bedroom with Cori and the girls. Cori must have told Sarah the same thing because she was rushing out of the bedroom after telling everyone good night. She headed straight to her bedroom to shower and go to bed.

Zel chuckled and shook his head. He glanced at Cori and Will. Will sat in the lounge chair beside the bed while Cori sat on the bed with the girls. Zel headed to the bedroom down the hall.

"Good luck with that one, boss." He mumbled.

Inside the bedroom Cori got comfortable on the bed. She didn't get under the comforter with the girls so it would be easy for her to get up after they fall asleep. She glanced over at Will who held up two books in his hands.

"So, which one should we start with?"

"The princess book!" Both girls shouted.

Will glanced at the books with a confused facial expression. "Which one is the princess book? This one looks like it's about a ninja and this one looks like it's about a warrior." He said.

"They're both princesses in their own way I think." Cori told him.

"Yeah, just because they don't look like it doesn't mean they're not a princess. In their heart they are one." Zela told him.

"One is a princess ninja like my sister and the other one is a princess warrior. That's what I'm going to be when I get bigger." Naya said with a head nod.

"Oooh, me too." Zela smiled with excitement.

Will looked over at Cori who had a big smile on her face. "It sounds like y'all already read these books."

"We did, Sarah had read them to us earlier before our nap." Naya said.

"You want me to read it to you again?" He asked.

"Yes, please."

"Okay, which princess book should I read first? The ninja princess or the warrior princess?"

Naya and Zela both looked at each other and started whispering amongst themselves. Cori and Will just smiled at them.

"Warrior princess!" They both yelled out and then giggled.

"Well, let's read about a warrior princess then." He opened the book and started reading.

Cori sat there as he read the book and looked from him to the girls. In that moment she realized how bad she wanted that life with Will. She wanted to be a family with him and raise their children together. She wanted to be a mother. The thought hit her hard. Cori never put much thought into having a family of her own. With the life she lived she didn't think it was possible, but now she was having second thoughts.

"This could be our life someday." She thought.

The smile on her face came naturally. A family of her own was now a goal she wanted to accomplish in life.

The stench of blood, piss, and shit reeked throughout the entire room. Felipe sat in the dark in the middle of the floor on his knees beaten, bruised, and bloody. He prayed for death to come for him soon. He didn't think he could take much more of the torture. Stepan and Alexei had taken turns torturing him for days. They had done things to cause him excruciating pain that he had never knew was possible.

Bright lights flipped on and flashed throughout the room. Felipe wanted to break down and cry. Not just from the lights hurting his sore and swollen eyes, but because he knew they came back to torture him some more. He now understood what the women and children he stolen felt when he had the same thing done to them.

"Oh Felipe, did you use the bathroom on yourself again?" Alexei asked. He stood a few feet away from Felipe with a white mask over his nose and mouth.

"He looks dead already." Felipe heard a female voice say.

"No, he's not dead yet, but he will be soon. We left that honor for you, baby girl." Stepan replied.

In that moment Felipe knew exactly who the female voice belonged to; Cori Romanov. This time he actually did cry. No sound came out though. His tears mixed with all the blood that leaked from his face.

"Are you crying, Mr. Gomez?" Cori questioned with a smirk.

"I think he is crying, niece." Alexei chuckled.

"That's funny to me seeing as how many women and little girls he most likely made cry. Did you stop when they asked you to, Mr. Gomez?"

Felipe head hung low. He was too afraid to look at her. He knew she was right about what he did. They used to cry and scream and all he did was laugh or beat them until they shut up. Now he regretted it all. His karma had finally come for him and it had a name; Romanov.

Cori glanced at the Niuweidao sword in her hand. She glared at Felipe when thoughts of men pointing their guns at her little sister. The shooters trying to kill her didn't faze her as much as it did when it came to Naya. She was an innocent child in all of this.

"Do you want me to end your suffering?" She asked.

Felipe slowly nodded his head. He was ready to die and face the consequences of his sins.

"All you have to do is tell me why. I want to hear it from your mouth."

"I... I... I did... I did it for money. There's a lot of... of money in the sex trafficking trade. I wanted parts of it." He stuttered.

Cori looked from her father to her uncle before she placed her attention back on him. "We already knew that's why you did that. You're a greedy scumbag that deserves to die for what you did to all those women and children. That is not what I wanted to know though."

Felipe finally looked up at her. He could barely see her from his swollen eyes. "What do you want to know? I tell you why I did it." He cried.

"I want you to tell me why you put a hit out on me and my little sister? Why did your men kill my babushka! (grandmother) Why did you think it was okay or safe to go against us?" She moved closer to him ignoring the smell that radiated off of him.

"My te, kto darit vzroslym muzhchinam, takim kak vy, koshmary tol'ko shepotom imeni Romanova! Kak ty smeyesh' prolivat' krov' Romanovykh!" (We are the ones who give grown men like you nightmares with just the whisper of the Romanov name! How dare you shed Romanov blood!) Cori shouted out before she swung the sword down on his shoulder. His whole right arm dropped to the floor.

"Ahhhhhhhh!" Felipe screamed out as blood poured from where his arm used to be.

"You shed Romanov blood and for that you will burn in hell."

He could feel himself getting light headed. He knew he was going to pass out any minute now. Her words confused him though. He didn't understand why she was saying them to him.

"No... no.... no, I didn't do it." He said as his eyes started to roll to the back of his head.

"What was that he said?" Stepan questioned.

"It wasn't me... I didn't put a hit out on you. Not me..." A hard and loud thud could be heard when he hit the concrete floor.

"Did he say he wasn't the one who put the hit out and killed our mother?" Alexei asked.

"He could be lying..." Stepan stated as he thought about it.

"He could be telling the truth as well. Either way he will die today." Cori swung the sword again and chopped Felipe's head clean off his shoulders. His head went rolling across the floor towards Alexei and Stepan. They glanced down at his it.

"We need to get out of here. We have a funeral to get to." Stepan said before he turned around and headed out the door.

Alexei and Cori followed close behind him. All three still had Felipe's last words on their mind. They weren't sure if he was telling the truth or not. Right now their main focus was putting Yuliya Romanov to rest.

~~~~~~~~~~~~~~~~~~~~~~

Once again the Romanov family was gathered together, but this wasn't a happy occasion. It was the day they had to bury and mourn the Matriarch of the family. Yuliya Romanov was one of the glues that held the family together. Now that she was gone that job was left solely on the shoulders of Alexei and Stepan.

The burial was filled with family, friends, and even associates of the Romanov family. Stepan had the security detail tripled for the funeral. Even though they felt they got the person responsible for the attack at the wedding, they still had to stay on alert.

"The cemetery is packed today." Alexei said as he stepped out of the limousine. After a quick glance around he reached back inside to help his wife out of the car.

"Some people are here to pay their respects and others are here to watch how we handle things." Stepan stated.

"Well, all they will see is the Romanov family with their heads held high. If they are looking for a reaction they won't get one. We're here to bury and celebrate the life of Yuliya. We've lost enough already and we won't show them any weaknesses where they can try to take from us again." Sofia, Alexei's wife stated before she placed her shades over her eyes.

Alexei and Stepan nodded in agreement. Sofia was always very soft spoken. When it came to family she made sure her voice was heard. It was one of the reasons Alexei fell in love with her.

Alyona, Monica, Heidi, and Katara walked over to them. They greeted each other.

"Has Cori, Will, and Naya arrived yet?" Alyona asked.

"I think they're in the limousine behind us. I'm about to go see now." Stepan said as he excused himself.

Inside the limousine Cori and Will was trying to explain to Naya what was going on. They had talked to her before they left the States, but she was still a little confused.

"Why will grandma be in a casket?" Naya asked Cori.

"Well, the casket is where her body will rest for now on."

"Her body?"

"Yes, grandma is gone to heaven and her body will stay here on earth."

Naya looked like she was trying to make sense of everything. "I don't want her to go to heaven yet. I want her to stay here with me. Can I just ask God to wait a little bit longer for her?"

Cori looked into her eyes and almost lost it. She had to turn her head to the side and take a deep breath. She wished that she had the power to bring Felipe back so that she could kill him again.

Will saw that Cori was struggling to answer Naya's last question. He decided to step in and help her out.

"Baby girl, things don't work like that with the big man upstairs. She's in a better place now."

The tears in Naya's eyes started to fall. "But I need her here with me. I need my nana." She cried.

Cori wrapped her arms around her and pulled her close. "He needed her more than we did, princess. As long as you hold her close in your heart then she would always be here with you."

There was a knock on the window of the limousine. Will unlocked the door and opened it before he stepped out. He and Stepan shook hands.

"They're having a hard time right not. Mostly Naya because you know Cori like to hold things in." He let him know.

Cori stepped out of the car with Naya in her arms. She was still crying, but it was a silent cry now. Cori passed her over to her father. When Naya saw his face she wrapped her arms around his neck.

"Daddy, nana went to heaven." She told him.

Stepan gently rubbed her back. "Yes, she did princess. Let's go say our goodbyes."

She lift her head off his shoulder and looked him in the eyes. "I don't want to say goodbye to nana."

Sofia walked over and rubbed her cheek. "We're not going to say goodbye then, sweetie. How about we just say see you later?"

"Are we going to see nana again someday?"

"Yes, but it won't be for a long time though."

Naya took a deep breath and nodded her head. "Okay, I'm ready to say see you later to nana."

Stepan placed her down on her feet. She grabbed Sofia's hand and let her lead her over to where the family was to be seated.

After everyone was in their seats the preacher started the service. Within fifteen minutes into the service a loud scream could be heard from the front row.

"Whyyyyy! Grandma, please come back!" Sasha cried out into her brother Dante's arms.

Cori looked over at her and rolled her eyes behind the big shades that covered her face. She knew that Sasha was going to pull something like this. She always had to make herself the center of attention. It was pathetic in Cori's opinion.

"Why is she screaming like that? Auntie Sofia said that we can see nana later." Naya said with her face scrunched up.

"Just ignore her, princess. She just want to be seen." Cori replied.

Sasha continued to be dramatic throughout the entire service. Even when it was over she still screamed and yelled with fake tears down her face. She didn't show that much appreciation to their grandmother when she was alive. She barely came around to visit or call her.

Cori glanced around the cemetery while everyone came to give their condolences to the family. She smiled a little when she saw Tari, Jason, and Skip walking towards her. Her head swung around to Will.

"Did you know they were coming?" She asked him.

"Yeah, I did."

"Hey girl, I'm so sorry for your loss." Tari said before she hugged her.

"Thank you, Tari. Why didn't you tell me that you were coming out here?"

Tari playfully rolled her eyes. "You are so nosey, Cori. I wanted to surprise you and come out here and show my support. I know this is a hard time for you. Plus, we're family now."

"Yeah and this family always have each other's back." Jason said before he hugged and kissed her on the cheek.

Skip did the same thing. "Aye, old man stop trying to steal my woman." Will joked.

"Shiiiiit, I'm brave but I'm not brave enough to tangle with this young Romanov." Skip chuckled.

They all laughed and talked some more. It made Cori feel good to know that her Chicago family had her back.

A few feet away some of the Romanov men stood around talking amongst themselves.

"Max, look at you boy. You've gotten so big." Alexei said to his youngest nephew who was also Elise's youngest son.

Max smiled a little. He looked up to his two uncles. He wanted to be just like them one day when he got older.

"How old are you now?" Stepan asked.

"I'm sixteen now, sir."

"He's becoming a young man." Alexei stated with a smile.

"Too bad my mom is not here to see him become a man." Dante said with a pat on Max's shoulder.

Stepan and Alexei looked at him with emotionless facial expressions at the mention of Elise.

"Yeah, too bad she'll be missing out." Stepan said.

Dante shook his head. "I still can't believe she just ran off and left everything behind. I mean, I knew her and our dad was having problems before she left, but I never thought she would leave her children behind. She could have at least called us to let us know she was okay."

"Mom hasn't cared about her children long before she ran off, Dante. She didn't even think to come to dad's funeral when he died. At this point I don't care where she is." Max spat.

Dante glared at him. "Max, do not speak that way about our mother. We don't know what she was dealing with to make her leave."

"I don't care because whatever it was it was more important to her than us."

"Stop it you two. This isn't a time where we need to be fighting." Sasha said to her older and younger brother.

"You're right, family is everything to us all. We shouldn't be fighting with each other." Dante said as he patted his brother on the shoulder.

"Let's head over to the venue for the repass, little brother."

"I was going to ride with our uncles." Max told him.

Dante looked from him to their uncles. "He's fine with us, Dante. We'll make sure he gets there." Stepan said.

"Okay, well Sasha let's go."

She gave each of her uncles a kiss on the cheek before she followed her brother to the car. Max watched them for a minute then turned back to his uncles.

"Uncle Stepan, I wanted to ask you something."

"You won't know the answer to your question if you don't ask it."

Max stood up straighter and looked him straight in the eye. "Can I come stay with you?"

Stepan was shocked by his question. "You want to come stay with me, why?"

"I think with my mom gone doing whatever; that I should live with you. Dante is my brother and I love him, but he's too busy to even pay attention to me being there. Plus, I would like to learn from you."

"Have you talked about this with your brother?"

He shook his head. "No, not yet. I wanted to get your permission first before I did that."

"Okay, well talk to your brother and you two come to an understanding about it. Then if you still want to you're more than welcome."

That made Max smile big. "Thanks uncle, I..."

Max was cut off by Stepan's phone going off. He stepped back to give his uncle some space to talk.

"Yes?" Stepan said into the phone.

"Boss, we got four unmarked cars heading in the direction of where you and the family are. Do you want us to cut them off and handle it?"

"Yes, don't let them get anywhere near here."

"You got it, boss."

Stepan hung up the phone and glanced around for Naya and Cori. He spotted them a few feet away talking to some familiar faces.

"Is there a problem, brother?" Alexei asked.

"Yes, get everyone in the cars and out of here now. We have some guest arriving."

Alexei pushed Max towards the limousine and grabbed his wife, daughter, her wife, and her friends as well. He led them all to the limousines and told the drivers to pull off. He turned back around to find his brother doing the same thing.

"What's going on now? I thought we got rid of our latest problem?"

Stepan shook his head. "Apparently, we were wrong brother. Either that or we had more than just one problem on our hands."

"Did our security team handle the situation?"

"They stopped them before they could make it to the area we were at. Two of the cars did get away though."

"Any survivors?"

"No, the ones that they hit are all dead. I'm going to have one of the tech guys look into finding out who the hell they are." Stepan stated.

"This is starting to really piss me off."

"You and me both, brother. It looks like I won't be bringing my baby girl home any time soon."

They got into the limousine that was waiting for them. The brothers both sat and thought deep on who could be out to shed more Romanov blood.

~~~~~~~~~~~~~~~~~~~~~~~~~~~~~~~~

The sound of his phone going off caused him to look at it. He picked it up and answered it on the second ring.

"This better be good news." He spoke into the phone.

"There was a problem with the plan."

"What type of problem?" He gritted out.

"They had the entire cemetery surrounded. They even had security set up a mile out."

He squeezed the phone in his hand. "What the hell are you telling me right now?"

The person on the other end sighed loudly into the phone. "We failed at hitting the targets and we lost four men in the process."

"You are all a bunch of fucking idiots! What the fuck am I paying you for?"

"Boss, we didn't know that they would have a set up like that."

"I told you to prepare for the unexpected when dealing with that family!" He took a breather.

"Get to the spot and make sure none of you are fucking followed." He snapped and then hung up the phone.

"This plan is proving to be more difficult than I thought." He mumbled and then threw his phone.

After the situation at the cemetery Cori, Will, Alyona, and everyone that came to Russia from Chicago hopped back on the plane to head back home. Most of them didn't even know there was a situation that had occurred or better yet almost occurred at the cemetery. Cori brought Naya back to Chicago with her and Will. She was only able to talk to her father for a few minutes before their plane pulled off. He mentioned that there was still some unresolved issues that needed to be handled before Naya could come back home. He also told her to stay on full alert until they find out what's going on.

Once the plane landed everyone said their goodbyes and went their separate ways. Naya was wide awake when they made it home. She was asking Will and Cori a million and one questions. Cori was starting to regret letting her eat those skittles on the plane. She was a little hyper than usual.

"Since it's still day time here, can Zela come over and play with me?"

"You're not tired just a little bit?" Will asked her.

"No, I don't feel tired at all." She smiled up at him.

Cori giggled and shook her head. "I'm not trying to be an instigator or anything, but you do owe them a movie date."

He looked over at her shocked. "Oh, that was a low blow."

"Will, we're sisters and we have to stick together." Naya said with a cheeky grin.

"I don't know what I am going to do with you two. Okay, go change into something more comfortable and I'll meet you back down here so we can go."

"Yayyy!" She ran up the stairs before either of them could stop her or Will could change his mind.

He glanced over at Cori when Naya was out of earshot. "You know I'm going to get you back for this right?"

She smirked at him. "I'm counting on it." She said and then walked up the stairs to help Naya.

Will stood back and watched her ass jiggle with each step. He shook his head to keep the naughty thoughts at bay. After pulling his phone out of his pocket, he dialed Zel up.

"You're back already, boss?" Zel asked when he answered the phone.

"Yeah, but hold off on that business talk right now. Is Zela with you today?"

"Yeah, she's over here talking about she's bored and when is her best friend coming back." They both chuckled.

"Naya is over here speaking that same tune. Since I still owe them a movie date, how about we take them today? Unless you already got something planned for y'all."

"Naw, I was just going to take her to get some pizza, but the movies sound like a better plan."

"We can actually do both. We're about to change clothes so by the time y'all get here we should be ready to go. We can pick my nephew up on the way there."

"Alright, see you then."

They ended the call and Will sent his sister Tari a quick text message.

Will: Kian, trying to kick it with his favorite uncle today?

Tari: I'll ask but you know the answer to that already.

Will: No, I don't. He's getting older he might don't want to hang out with me anymore.

Tari: Lol yeah right!

Tari: He said yes... I told you.

Will: Tell him I'll be there in about thirty to forty minutes at the most.

Tari: Okay and tell Cori... never mind I'll just text or call her myself.

Will: What you don't want me in y'all business?

Tari: Exactly! Nosey big head dude! Lol

He laughed out loud after reading her last text message. He replied to it and then headed upstairs to change out of the suit he was wearing.

Down the hallway in Naya's bedroom Cori was helping her pick out an outfit. A few days after they brought her to Chicago with them, she and Cori had gone shopping for a new wardrobe. That still didn't stop Naya from trying to wear clothes that didn't match.

"Naya, you can't wear shorts it's starting to get chilly outside."

"You wore shorts outside the other day." Naya replied with a knowing look.

Cori rolled her eyes and rubbed her forehead. "Okay, well do as I say and not as I do then."

When she just stood there and stared at her Cori sighed. "That didn't work?"

Naya shook her head. "Only when daddy says it."

"Yeah, you're right. Let me get him on the phone then." Cori played like she was reaching for her phone.

"Noooo... okay, I'll listen don't call daddy!" She whined.

"You promise to listen and do as I say?"

"Yes, just please don't call daddy. I promised him that I'll be a good girl. I don't want him to think I was being bad." She pleaded.

"Okay, I won't call him then. We agree that you can't wear shorts though, right?"

"Yes."

"Good, let's find you something warm and comfortable."

"No sweaters please."

"Okay, no sweaters." Cori searched through her closet. She pulled out a pair of dark blue skinny jeans, a light pink colored long sleeve shirt with princess written in glitter on the front, and a dark pink leather jacket.

"How does this look?"

Naya tapped her chin and looked at the outfit. "I like it."

"Good, now let's get you changed before he leaves you."

"Will wouldn't leave me. He's not mean like that."

Cori chuckled. "You're right, he wouldn't leave you."

After Naya put her clothes on Cori grabbed her pink Uggs boots with the bow on them. Once her outfit was complete she did a twirl in front of her.

"How do I look?"

"You look beautiful as usual." They heard Will say from the doorway.

Naya blushed. "Thank you, Will. You look beautiful too."

Cori glanced at him and laughed. "I was going to go with handsome, but you're right he does look beautiful."

Will glanced down at the burgundy Nike sweatpants suit that he had on. When he wanted to be comfortable and dress down he always leaned towards sweatpants.

"Y'all are going to stop trying to tag team me all the time."

"We just want you to know that you're beautiful to us." Cori smirked.

"Yeah, you're beautiful to us." Naya co-signed.

Before he could respond the doorbell rang. A few minutes later Sarah was yelling up the stairs.

"Mr. Cooper, Mr. Zel and Ms. Zela are here!"

Will walked down the stairs as Naya and Cori followed close behind him. "Sarah, I told you to call me Will."

She nodded. "I'm sorry, I forget sometimes."

"That's okay, there's nothing to be sorry about."

"Zela!"

"Naya!"

The girls ran to each other and hugged as if they hadn't seen each other in years. Zel shook his head because it had only been a few days since they last seen one another.

"They are so extra and I love it. It reminds me of Katara and Heidi." Cori stated with a smile.

Will turned to her and gave her a kiss on the lips. "We'll be back in a few hours."

"Okay, while y'all are gone Sarah and I will try not to throw any wild party." She responded and got a laugh out of all of them.

Cori watched them walk out the door and get in the truck. After they pulled off she closed and locked the door before heading upstairs to change her clothes.

Once she changed into something more comfortable, she headed downstairs to the kitchen to grab a snack. She needed to talk to her father about what happened at the cemetery. After she grabbed a small bowl of fruit from out of the fridge; she sat down at the table and called him up.

"I knew you would be calling me soon." Stepan stated as soon as he answered the phone.

"That was a given after what happened today. What exactly was it that happened today?"

"Are you all back at home?"

"Yes."

"Where is Naya?"

"Will took her, Zela, and Kian to the movies."

"That's good, the more she's distracted the less questions she'll have." He replied.

Cori chuckled a little. "I don't know about that. Naya is a curious little girl."

"Just like her big sister was when she was little." There was a short pause before Stepan spoke again.

"Someone tried to do another attack again at the cemetery."

"Do we know who it was this time? Were they connected to Felipe?" Cori questioned.

"I had some of my people run the finger prints of the dead men. They didn't seem to have any connection to Felipe or Emiliano. I did find something more alarming though."

"What?"

"They were all Italian. So far we had been dealing with other Russians, Felipe was Hispanic, and now we're dealing with the Italians. I don't know if they all are connected and joined forces to try and take us out or what. I do know that we need to find the head to all of this and chop it off."

"Russians, Hispanics, and Italians working together. Last time that happened we were the ones who brought them all together to make money. Somebody brought them together to take us out, but who? After the situation with Aunt Elise and Trent's murder things had calmed down." Cori stated as if she was in deep thought trying to piece everything together.

Stepan sighed. "I'm starting to think that was just the calm before the storm."

152

"Do you think that Elise was working with someone else?"

He thought about the dream he had been having about Elise and his late wife Cynthia.

"You will reap what you sow, Stepan! Romanov blood lasts forever!" She shouted in their native Russian tongue.

"The worst is yet to come. Be wary of the company you keep and the things going on around you. Be sure to always protect the girls. Naya is so beautiful. You did well by giving her a family and good life. She's so precious and innocent. She has a spirit like Cori, which means she's a fighter as well." Cynthia smiled.

"Daddy, are you still there?" Cori asked getting his attention.

"Uh yes, I'm here. I don't think she was working with anyone else. We had gotten rid of everybody that helped her try to kill you. The way things are going though, I could be wrong. I'll go over all those details again to see if I might of missed anything." He stated.

"I thought about what Elise's objective was when she tried to kill me. She wanted to hurt you the way she thought you hurt her with killing her Italian lover."

"I wasn't the one who killed him though."

"Yeah, but she didn't know that until you told her right before you killed her. Whoever is doing this now has the same objective by trying to hurt you by killing me and Naya. We need to find out who your enemies are in order to find out who is behind this."

"Wait, Elise didn't know I wasn't responsible for her lover's death. I'm starting to think how weird it was that her husband was killed in that car crash not too long after her death. Would it be crazy to think that it's all connected?"

Cori leaned back in her seat. "At this point we can't count out anything. It all could be connected or it could be something completely different."

"I don't like not being in the know." Stepan responded.

"I don't like it either."

"I'm going to go back over everything that happened in the last year. At the moment this person or people have been one step ahead of us the entire time. It's time I remind everyone who I am."

"The Grim Reaper is back again?"

"I don't think he's ever left."

Cori smiled at his response. "Let's hope someone prays for the souls he takes."

"Yes, let's hope."

Cori ended the phone call with her father. She would make a few calls of her own to try and get some answers to their questions as well. Something about what her father said lingered in her head. Whoever was behind all of this had been a step ahead of them the entire time. That to her meant one thing; inside job. It had to be someone close to them running the show or someone who knew enough on how they operated in order to pull it off.

"Who are you?" She thought.

Her phone rang after she placed it back down on the table. She picked it up and recognized the number all too well.

"Mr. Acardi, how can I help you?" She asked once she answered. Acardi was a top client of hers. She had done many hits for him over the years and had been paid exceptionally well.

"Ah Ms. Romanov, how are you this evening? I hope you got the flowers I sent to you in Russia. I want to once again give you my deepest condolences on the loss of your grandmother."

"Thank you, Mr. Acardi. I did receive the flowers. They were very beautiful."

"I'm glad they made it in time. I called you because I had been hearing things through our mutual associates."

Cori lifted a brow at his words. "What have you heard?"

"Well, I heard that your family had been having a pest problem. I want you to know that if you need anything please don't hesitate to ask. You are a very important and special asset to me and my organization. You had helped me out many of times. I would like to extend that to you as well. After all it is because of you that I am alive and free now."

She smirked at that thought. "Thank you for that, Mr. Acardi. I will remember your words."

"Yes, anything you need no matter what it is just let me know."

"I will... wait, have you heard anything about who the head pest might be?"

"No, I'm sorry I do not know. If I did I would have let you know as soon as I found out. I have been keeping ears and eyes out there though."

"Your generosity will not go unnoticed." She told him.

"All you have to do is say the word and anything in my power will be yours to do with as you please."

A wide grin spread across her face. "I do have something I might need a little help on."

"Name it and it's done."

Once they discussed what she needed from him they ended the call. Cori sat back in the chair with a satisfied smirk on her face. If things played out how she wanted it, she'll find out the truth and everything she needed to know soon enough.

~~~~~~~~~~~~~~~~~~~~~~~

A hour and a half later Will, Zel, and the kids had just left the movie theater. While in the truck the kids went back and forth on which pizza place they wanted to go to. Everyone decided on 'The Art of Pizza' restaurant. Upon arrival Zel went in first to check the restaurant out. Once he saw that it was safe for them to enter they got out the truck.

"I want a deep dish pizza." Zela said once everyone sat down at the table.

"What's a deep dish pizza?" Naya asked.

"It's a pizza that's baked in a pan and the toppings are like two or three inches thick. It's good pizza." Kian explained.

Naya looked over at Will. "I want that kind of pizza."

He chuckled. "Okay, what do y'all want on it?"

"Cheese!"

"Pepperoni!"

"Sausage!"

All three kids yelled out. "Does it matter if it's on the same pizza?" Zel asked them.

"Nope."

A waitress came over and took their order. Will got the kid's pizza and then a regular pizza for them. For their drinks he got them juice instead of soda. As he and Zel watched the kids while also watching their surroundings they talked amongst themselves.

"How are things going with her mom?" He asked only loud enough for Zel to hear him.

"It's still the same. Instead of her thinking about Zela's best interest at heart she's being selfish. She only thinks about herself." He kept his facial expression neutral even though the thought of it made him mad.

"I think everything will work out for the best."

"I know it will because I'm going to do whatever I need to for my daughter."

"Have she said anything to you?" Will nodded over towards Zela. The three kids were lost in their own little world not paying them any attention.

"She doesn't say much about her mom when she's with me. Only time she does speak on the situation is when it's time for me to drop her off over there."

"What does she say?"

"That she wants to stay with me. I told her that I'm working on it."

They ended that conversation when the waitress arrived with their food. Watching them made Will even more anxious to have a little one of his own. A mini him and Cori was just what the world needed whether they agreed or not.

They ate until they were full and then left the restaurant. Will had Zel drop Kian off at home first before they headed back to the house. By the time they had arrived Naya and Zela had already decided that they were going to have a sleepover. Zel was about to tell Zela she couldn't stay without asking permission first, but Will told him it was cool. He figured that it would be payback to Cori for reminding Naya about the movie date.

Before they could get all the way through the front door they heard music blasting. Zel and Will looked at each other already knowing what it was.

"Did my sister and Sarah throw a wild party for real?" Naya asked Will.

"I don't know, but let's go crash it." He replied.

"Yessss!" She and Zela screamed as they rushed into the house.

When Will and Zel made it to the den where the music was coming from they stopped dead in their tracks. Cori and her friends Katara, Heidi, and her cousin Alyona and her wife Monica were all dancing up on each other. A few of them had drinks in their hands taking sips as they danced. They even had Sarah in there with them laughing and dancing. All of the women seemed to be having a good time.

Will's eyes were trained on his baby. She was backing her butt up into Katara. When her eyes landed on him she smiled and stood up a little.

"There goes my maintenance man!" Cori yelled out.

He glanced around and then pointed at himself. "You're talking about me?" He questioned.

She nodded and slowly made her way over to him. "Yes, I'm talking about you."

Will rubbed his jaw and chuckled. "Well, I've fixed and cleaned out a few pipes in my day." He smirked.

Zela leaned over towards Naya and whispered in her ear. "What's a maintenance man?"

Naya shrugged. "I think it's someone who fix and clean stuff."

"Oh okay... wait, I didn't know Will was a maintenance man who fixed and cleaned stuff."

"Me either, girl. Adults are so weird sometimes."

"Let's sneak over to that table where they got the snacks. Maybe they won't see us sense they're too busy having fun." Zela suggested.

Naya rubbed her hands together and smiled. "Let's do it."

While the girls snuck over to the snacks, Will had pulled Cori out of the room for some privacy. Everyone else continued to enjoy themselves.

Zel couldn't keep his eyes off of Katara. Her smooth hazelnut brown skin glistened as she worked up a little sweat from dancing. His eyes roamed all over here body. From her plump juicy gloss covered lips, down to her nice size breast, and her thick thighs. When she turned around and wiggled her ass, he bit down on his bottom lip. It wasn't too big, but it damn sure wasn't small.

"Is it a reason why you keep staring at me, Mr. Chocolate man?" Katara said without turning around.

"Are you referring to me?" He asked.

She turned around and walked up on him. "You're the only other man in here. Will had already disappeared somewhere with Cori."

"Why chocolate man?"

Katara smirked as she stared him straight in the eyes. "I called you that because your skin is the perfect shade of chocolate." She touched his cheek and smiled.

He leaned in close to her. "Since you touched me it's only fair that I get to touch you too."

"I guess that's fair."

"Can I take you out to dinner one day?"

"Will you touch me on that day?" She flirted.

Zel smirked. "Say yes and find out."

"Yes."

He pulled out his phone and handed it to her. "Put your number in my phone and I'll call you with the details."

Katara accepted the phone and put her number in it before she passed it back to him. "You better not stand me up."

"I'll be crazy to do that."

"You'll be surprised how many times it's happened to me."

"Well, don't compare them to me. I plan on showing you things you've never experienced before."

"I'm going to hold you to that." She said before she turned and walked away. She made sure to put a little more bounce in her ass just in case he was watching.

Zel grinned as he watched her walk over to her friends. They started speaking in whispers. When they glanced his way and giggled he knew they were talking about him.

Will and Cori had finally made their way back into the den. They had silly grins plastered on their face. Everyone looked at them and started laughing.

"What?" Cori asked as she sat down next to her cousin.

"You two are nasty." She giggled.

"We didn't do anything, but talk." Cori lied. The huge smile never left her face.

"Stop lying, girl. You just got your pipes fixed." Monica said.

Cori blushed. "Okay, I might have just gotten them a little tweaked."

"Monica, I know you and Alyona not talking. I know you two weren't talking about the clouds in the sky when y'all disappeared an hour ago for like thirty minutes." Heidi commented.

Monica eyed her wife. "Oh, I was cleaning my baby's pipes. I had to make sure they were shiny new."

It was Alyona's turn to blush. Sarah walked over to where they sat. She had enough fun for the night and was now tired.

"Cori, do you need me to take the girls upstairs to prepare for bed?" She asked.

At the mention of the girls everyone turned in their direction. Naya and Zela were seated off in the corner of the room. They had a pile of snacks in front of them. They were both in their own world snacking that they hadn't noticed everyone staring at them.

"I forgot they were in here with us." Heidi said.

"Yeah, me too." Katara said.

Cori stood up and walked over to them. "Are you two little thieves enjoying yourself?"

They looked up at her with widened eyes. They had finally been caught. Naya placed the chocolate donut that she was about to eat down.

"Thieves are people who take stuff that doesn't belong to them. The snacks was sitting out for everyone to enjoy." She said and smiled up at her sister.

Cori squint her eyes a little and then chuckled. "Okay, that's true but it's time for you two to go to bed. Now get up and go upstairs with Sarah so she can give you a bath. I'll be up there soon to tuck you in."

"Okay." They both said as they stood up.

"Are you going to read us a story?" Naya asked.

"Yes, but I get to choose this time because you chose last time."

"Okay, but as long as it's about princesses. I have to read up on my kind."

"Yeah, me too." Zela agreed.

"What are y'all kind?" Katara asked after she overheard them.

"Princesses." They both replied.

She smiled as she watched them walk out the room with Sarah. She felt someone staring at her and glanced around the room. Her eyes landed on Zel. He winked at her and then continued the private conversation he was having with Will.

"Are you guys sure you don't want to crash here tonight?" Cori asked them.

"No, we'll be fine. We caught a lyft here." Alyona replied.

"I can take you ladies home if you need me to." Zel suggested.

"We don't want to intrude on your night." Monica told him.

"You won't be intruding at all. I was about to head out anyway."

"Okay thank you, Zel." Alyona, Monica, and Heidi said.

Katara eyed him for a minute. "Yeah, thanks."

"It's not a problem."

As they were getting their stuff ready for them to leave, Alyona's phone beeped. She glanced at the phone and read the text that had come through.

"Sasha just landed in Chicago. We should be home by the time she arrives there."

Cori rolled her eyes at the mention of their other cousin. Alyona caught it and sighed.

"How about the three of us do lunch sometime soon?" She asked.

Cori glanced around her as if she didn't know she was speaking to her. "Are you talking to me?"

"Yes, I'm talking to you."

"Uh, no I'm sorry I'm going to have to decline the invitation."

"Come on Cori, please." She begged.

"Ugh, okay fine. The only reason I'm agreeing to this is because I'm still high from the orgasm I just had. I'm in a good mood so leave before I change my mind."

Alyona kissed her on the cheek and then headed to the front door. She knew Cori was serious and wanted to get out of there before she really did change her mind.

After everybody said their goodbyes Cori and Will were left alone downstairs. He pulled her to him.

"Did you have a good time with your girls?"

She nodded. "Yes, I wasn't expecting them to come over here. They popped up and said they wanted to spend some time with me. I think it was Alyona's idea. She knew how close I was to our grandmother. I think she felt like I needed to be surrounded by love, positivity, and good memories."

He kissed her forehead. "You have a great cousin and great friends."

"Yes, I do. I'm really lucky to have them all. In this life we live in we don't get to have many friends that we can trust." She rubbed his jaw before kissing his lips.

"After all this bullshit with the attacks is handled and over, I have plans for us." Will stated.

"What kind of plans?"

"We'll discuss them when this is all over."

"Okay."

They headed upstairs to take a shower together. After their shower Cori had gone to Naya's bedroom to check on the girls. They were sound asleep in the bed knocked out. She kissed both girls on the forehead then slowly made her way out the room.

"I guess I owe them two stories next time." She mumbled before going back to the master bedroom.

"Were they already sleep?" Will asked when she climbed in the bed next to him. He immediately wrapped his arms around her and pulled her close.

"Yes, they were knocked out."

"You know they're not going to let you forget that you owe them a story, right?"

She giggled. "I already know that I'm going to have to read them two stories next time. Kids always remember what you said or did and didn't do. They always have amnesia when the tables are turned. I learned a lot being around Naya."

Will chuckled. "Just imagine how our kids would be."

That made her smile. "I do imagine it. I imagine it a lot."

"That makes two of us then." He kissed her forehead.

They both fell asleep cuddled up in each other's arms.

Chapter 11

~The next day in Russia~

Stepan sat in his office going over the meetings he had set up with a few of his associates. His life was hectic at the moment, but he was used to not cracking under pressure. That was something his enemies always hated about him.

The sound of his phone going off caught his attention. When he glanced at the screen and saw a picture of his girls, a smile graced his face.

"Isn't it early in the morning out there?" He asked when he answered the phone. His smile turned to a grin because he already knew what her response would be.

"The early bird always gets the worm." Cori replied.

"That is true."

"I was getting ready for my morning workout and decided to call you."

He chuckled. "Is this your way of checking up on me and making sure I'm okay?"

"Maybe... are you okay?"

He knew that she was referring to his mother's death and not just the enemy that lurked in the shadows. When he thought about it, he never really had time to mourn the loss of his mother. His focus had mostly been on protecting his daughters from the unknown enemy.

"I'm doing as best as I can be at the moment. There will be a time when I can properly mourn my loss, but now isn't it. It's too much going on at this time."

"Have any leads come up yet?"

"No, but I have a meeting in a few hours. I'm hoping someone can help shed some light on things."

"Cori is that daddy on the phone? Can I speak to him, please?" He heard Naya ask from the other end.

"Yes, hold on a second." Cori handed her the phone.

"Hi, Papa." Naya greeted when she got on.

"Hello, printsessa." (princess)

"How was your day?"

Stepan grinned. "My day was just okay, sweetheart. It's usually better when you're here."

"Do you need me to come home, Papa? I don't want you to be sad or lonely." She pouted.

"No printsessa, I'll be fine. I want you to enjoy your time out there with your sister and Will."

"I am and I'm having fun with my best friend Zela too. Do you remember I told you about her when I was home?"

"Yes, I remember. I'm glad that you met a new friend out there."

"When I come home can she come with me to visit?" Naya asked and smiled over at Zela. She was standing a few feet away tying her shoes up. They were getting ready to go work out with Cori.

"We'll have to check with her parents first, sweetheart."

"Okay, I love you daddy. If you get sad or lonely call me, okay?"

Stepan chuckled. "I will do that. I love you too, printsessa."

Naya passed Cori back the phone. "She's like a little lady." Cori giggled.

"She really is... I love you both with everything in me. Stay safe and tell Will continue to keep his word."

After a few more words Stepan ended the call with his daughter. Right when he was about to stand up and exit his office, his phone rang again. This time the caller's name that popped up didn't put a smile on his face like the last one did. Mostly because he knew this wasn't about to be a pleasant phone call.

"I'm guessing that you talked to your brother about his living arrangements?" He got right to the point.

"You told Max that he could come and stay with you?" Dante asked. He tried not to let too much of his anger show. He knew his uncle's reputation and Stepan wasn't one to accept disrespect no matter who you are.

"He asked if he could and I told him yes. My nephew would always be welcome into my home same as you and your sister." Stepan leaned back in his chair with the phone placed firmly at his ear.

"Uncle, you know why he wants to come there?"

"I do."

"He wants in the life and Max isn't ready for that."

"You are correct, Dante. Max is sixteen years old and he's not prepared enough to defend himself if ever he need to. Whether you all realize it or not he has Romanov blood flowing through his veins. Because of that alone he

172

could have a target on his back. It was irresponsible for your parents not to help prepare him for the challenges life might throw his way."

"Not everybody wanted their child to grow up to be a killer." As soon as the words left Dante's mouth he regretted them. He was speaking out of anger. He didn't want his little brother anywhere near the lifestyle his uncles lived. In a way he was being a hypocrite. It was because of the lives his uncles both lived that he and his family were able to live a comfortable lifestyle as well. Stepan and Alexei made sure their entire family lived good. It was one of the reasons they couldn't and wouldn't understand Elise's betrayal.

Stepan smirked and then leaned forward with his elbows rested on the desk. "You are correct again, Dante. Keep this up because you're on a roll. Yes, my daughter is one of the world's most deadliest killers to ever walk the earth. She's trained to protect herself, but most importantly Dante, she's trained to survive. I knew the blood that runs through my veins runs through hers as well. I knew that I wouldn't always be around to protect her. So, yes I gave my child the skills to protect herself. As parents we all do what has and needs to be done for our children. Well, at least some of us do."

"Wouldn't that be putting him directly in front of the craziness by doing this?"

"It just depends on how you see it. Max need to know how to protect himself and the ones he love."

"He's not ready for this, Uncle Stepan."

"You're missing an important detail, Dante."

"What is that?"

"This was all Max's idea. You may not be ready for him to learn, but he is. Again, he's always welcome here. You should try to understand why he wants to do this instead of trying to force him not to." Stepan left him with those final words and then hung up. There was nothing else that needed to be said.

Stepan stood to his feet and headed out of the office. He needed to prepare for his meeting. Dante's concerns were just that; his. He had more important issues to deal with at the moment.

~~~~~~~~~~~~~~~~~~~~~~~~~~~~

When the back door opened up, Stepan stepped out of the car. He glanced over to the other side and watched as his brother did the same. Alexei made his way over to his brother and stood beside him. They glanced up at the top of the three story building and then at each other.

Stepan nodded. "Is our men already in position?" He asked.

"Yes, we have a few on the roof and also on the surrounding roofs. Some of our men are already located inside of the building as well. We've come prepared, brother."

"As we always do. Let's go get this over with. I hope that we're able to learn something new from this meeting."

Alexei smirked as they made their way towards the door led by one of their men. "We always learn something new because we know to pay attention to everyone and everything. You meant to say that you hope we learn something that's beneficial to what we're dealing with now."

Stepan chuckled. "You've always been the direct one."

"That I am."

The door to the warehouse opened up and a big guy stood before them. The brothers looked at each other and smiled. It was as if they were communicating with each other without actually speaking.

"I see that Chugunkin has gotten some new and improved help." Alexei thought with a slight chuckle. The last time he and Endar Chugunkin had crossed paths; Alexei had killed mostly all of his security team. After that Endar never got on his bad side again. If one man could wipe out close to twenty well trained men in less than ten minutes, he wasn't the man you wanted to be enemies with.

"No weapons gets pass the door. I ask that if you have any on your person that you hand them over, please." The big guy that stood at the door stated. He was nervous to request such a thing from the Romanov men. Everyone in Russia and other parts of the world knew of them. He didn't want to piss them off in any way.

Stepan eyed him for a minute before he spoke. The smirk that crossed his face had the man even more nervous. He thought that he might shit himself any second.

"We don't have any weapons on us because we don't need them. Our reputation speaks for itself. You are more than welcome to still check though."

He feverishly shook his head. "That won't be necessary sir." He stepped aside and granted them entry inside.

"Thank you."

Alexei glanced around and then focused at the table that sat in the center of the room. Seated at the table were three of the other top heavy hitters in Russia. They weren't as powerful or rich as the Romanovs, but they all had made a name for themselves that got them close to the top of the game.

As they made their way over to the table all three men stood to their feet. Stepan and Alexei nodded their heads and all five men took a seat.

"Stepan, Alexei, it is good to see you." Boris Orlov greeted with a head nod.

"I always heard that it's good for me to be seen because when I'm not people tend to mysterious die." Alexei chuckled.

"Which I'm sure that's where you got the nickname Ghost from." Boris said with a grin.

Alexei nodded. "Yes, that is true."

Stepan's eyes landed on a man by the name of Gervasi Petrov. The two of them had crossed paths in the pass on multiple occasions. The only reason why Gervasi was still able to live, was because Stepan enjoyed the fear he sensed from him whenever they were in the same room. Stepan had always been unpredictable and never showed his hand. Every day that Gervasi woke up he never knew if that would be his last day on earth.

"Stepan and Alexei, I would like to give my condolences on the loss of your mother." Endar said.

"Thank you... that's part of the reason we are here today." Alexei stated.

All three men glanced at each other. Gervasi was the first one to speak up. "I thought that we were here to discuss Emiliano and his businesses. Now that he's gone we should decide on who takes over his territory."

Stepan chuckled. "The Romanovs have no desire for any of Emiliano's territory. It didn't bring him much money which I'm sure was why he decided to work with Felipe in the first place."

Alexei watched all the men's reaction to that information. He wanted to see who knew about the deal Emiliano made with Felipe. They all knew the rule. No sex trafficking allowed. Any violation of that rule was punished by death.

"Felipe only deals in sex trafficking of women and little girls." Boris gritted out. Just like Stepan and Alexei he despised women and children being taken from their families and homes to become sex slaves.

"Exactly and Emiliano wanted in on that business. He decided that he didn't care about the rules. That is why he is no longer with the living." Alexei stated.

"Skatert'yu doroga!" (Good riddance) Boris spat.

"As I'm sure you all know about the attempted attacks on my daughters lives..." Stepan said changing the subject.

All three men nodded. "Yes and I don't understand who could be more stupid to do something like that. Not only because of who you are, but because of who your oldest daughter Cori is. No offense to you Stepan or even you Alexei, but she's the most deadliest Romanov there is. Who in their right mind would want to tangle with her?" Endar honestly looked confused.

Stepan smiled. "No offense taken. She had built up an amazing reputation for herself."

"You should be proud."

"I am."

"I now understand this meeting. I would like to be the first to go on record stating that I had nothing to do with the attacks. We do great business together and quite frankly, I enjoy life and would like to keep living it." Boris stated as he stared both Stepan and Alexei directly in the eyes.

"The same here... I don't know anything about who could have done it. I do know that I wasn't involved." Endar said.

All eyes landed on Gervasi. He looked around at them and shrugged his shoulders.

"Do not look over this way. We may have had our differences in the past, but I would never try anything this stupid. It wasn't me and I don't know who it was." He told them.

Stepan glanced over at his brother and they both stood to their feet. "Thank you gentlemen for your time. A little friendly advice; be careful on the streets of Russia for a little while. Things are going to get a little messy."

"Noted." They all said at the same time.

Once Alexei and Stepan were back in the car, they pulled off. Alexei looked over at Stepan and noticed that he seem to be in deep thought.

"Do you believe that none of them had anything to do with it?"

"Oddly, I do believe them. I'll still have them watched though. I don't want to underestimate anyone at this time. My daughters' lives depend on it."

Alexei leaned back in the seat in deep thought. He agreed with his brother on believing that they may have not had anything to do with the attacks. He also agreed that underestimating anyone right now could be dangerous. He thought about it as if it was his daughter in the position his nieces were in. He would move heaven and earth to find the ones responsible just like he and Stepan plan to do for Cori and Naya.

"I'm sure all would be revealed soon and when it is we'll move accordingly." He stated.

~~~~~~~~~~~~~~~~~~~~~~~~~~~~~~~~~~~~~

On the other side of the world, Cori strolled into a nice little restaurant in downtown Chicago. She had finally agreed to meet with Alyona and Sasha for lunch. She had thought about declining on Alyona again, but decided against. Cori reminded herself that she needed to have a few words with Sasha. She didn't get the chance to do so when they were in Russia for the funeral because her focus was on her sister and her father at that time.

Cori glanced around the restaurant until her eyes landed on her cousins. She made her way over to the table and took a seat.

"Cori, I'm glad you made it." Alyona greeted as soon as her butt touched the seat.

"I told you that I would."

"I know, but you're always so busy and I know how plans could change quickly for you." Alyona looked at both her cousins. Neither of them had yet to acknowledge the other. Sasha had her face in her phone either scrolling social media or texting. Alyona nudged her a little. When she looked up from her phone, Alyona nodded towards Cori.

"Sasha, look Cori is here."

"Oh, hey cousin." She greeted with a fake smile.

"Hey Sasha."

An awkward silence fell over the table. Alyona called over the waitress and they ordered their drinks and food. She had small talk with both of them until their food arrived.

"So, Cori how is Naya doing? I saw her for a minute the other day, but you know I was a little tipsy."

Cori smiled at her thinking about how much fun they had the other day. "She's doing a lot better. She misses our father and grandma. You know she's never been away from them that long."

"I feel so sad for her. I know we're hurting too, but just imagine what her little mind and emotions are going through."

"Yeah, me too. Will and I try to keep her occupied so she won't think about it much. Zela, her new best friend is a lot of help as well."

"I'm glad she's got someone her age to play with. The other kids in our family are a little bit older than her."

"They might not want to play with her much because she's a little rough around the edges." Sasha said before taking a bite of her salad.

Alyona and Cori stared at her with different facial expressions. Alyona was shocked that she had said something like that. Cori on the other hand was pissed. She was sick of Sasha and her little slick comments about her little sister.

"What the hell do you mean by that?" She glared at her while tapping her fingers on the table.

"Cori..."

"No Alyona, let her answer the question. I would love to hear the meaning behind her statement."

Sasha glanced at Alyona and then at Cori. She swallowed the thump that seemed to had gotten caught in her throat.

"I just meant that Naya likes to play differently than the other kids. She's more of a fighter and plays rough. They might not like that. That's all I was saying."

"Are you sure that's all because you always seem to have a lot to say about and to her?"

Her face showed her confusion. "What are you talking about?"

"Okay, first let's start with the statement you just made. I don't believe for one minute that's why the kids and Naya don't really play with each other. I think it's more of what Alyona stated. They are in different age groups so their interests are a lot different. Naya is not rough around the edges. The way her and Zela play proves your comment to be bullshit."

"I was just..."

Cori put her hand up to stop her from speaking. Sasha closed her mouth immediately. "I don't care what you were about to say. I'm not done talking. Now, let's move along to the comments you made to her about my father not really caring about her and would most likely send her back to the people who hurt her."

Alyona's mouth fell open in shock. "Please tell me you didn't say that to her?" Alyona had been through something similar to what Naya had gone through. It was worse for Naya because she loss both her parents when she was taken from her home by sex traffickers. That horrible situation was where Cori had found Naya. So she knew how scared and hurt Naya probably was when Sasha said those words to her. Cori had only told Alyona a little of what Sasha had said. She didn't mention that part of it.

"I... I... I didn't." She stuttered.

"Oh so you're saying that Naya made that up? I know that's bullshit because she cries just thinking about that time in her life." Cori leaned forward on the table and stared her directly in the eyes.

"If I find out that you said anything else to my sister that hurts her, I'll forget that you're my blood. She's a little kid that had already been through a lot of bullshit as it is. She doesn't need the people who are supposed to love and care about her to try and hurt her too." Cori stood to her feet. She dropped some money on the table to cover the bill and tip.

"I'm sorry..." Sasha said.

She cut her eyes at her. "You will be if you ever hurt my sister." She calmly stated.

Cori made eye contact with Alyona. "Lunch is on me today. Enjoy the meal and drinks." She then made her way out of the restaurant with her head held high.

After Cori had left Alyona could barely make eye contact with Sasha. She tried to explain to her what was said and that she was sorry, but Alyona wasn't trying to hear it. No one could truly know the pain and suffering women and children that are taken, beaten, and raped go through unless they had been through it themselves. She felt what Sasha said was horrible and inconsiderate.

Alyona was now starting to rethink the idea of Sasha staying with her while she was out there. She was also starting to see that she had a lot of similar traits like her mother.

Chapter 12

~A few weeks later~

Cori had some business to handle for a client while Will was busy with handling some business of his own. They were going to keep Naya at the house with Sarah and her security detail, but Alyona had begged Cori to let Naya come spend some time with her and Monica. They wanted to take her to the mall and have a fun day with her. Cori was skeptical about it at first because she didn't want her around Sasha. Alyona had assured her that she would keep close eyes on her and monitor any conversation between her and Sasha. She gave in and agreed but let her know that there would be a team in the shadows following them. Her first and most important priority was Naya's safety.

When Alyona arrived to pick Naya up, Cori had already had a talk with Naya. She was excited to hang out with Alyona and Monica. She wasn't too thrilled about seeing Sasha though.

"Remember, you don't have to talk to her if you don't want to." Cori told her.

"I don't want to." Naya replied in a matter of fact tone.

"Okay, I'll let Alyona know. Come on she's waiting downstairs for you."

She reached her hand out for her to take. When she did they both headed downstairs together.

"Am I spending a night with them?"

"No, Will or I will pick you up later when we're done working."

"Okay."

"Hi Naya, are you excited to hang out with us today?" Alyona asked when they came down.

Naya smiled up at her big cousin. "Yes! Cori said that you're taking me to the mall."

"Yup and then we're going to go have dinner."

"I can't wait!" She squealed with excitement. She liked spending time with Alyona whenever she came around.

"Bye Cori, I love you!" She waved to her and then grabbed Alyona's hand.

While Alyona laughed Cori shook her head. "She was a little too happy to leave me." She mumbled.

She felt a strong pair of arms wrap around her waist. "She's just happy to hang out with her big cousin. You know she adores you." Will whispered in her ear.

Cori turned around to face him. She kissed him and then stared him in the eyes. "Are you about to head out?"

"Yes..." He glanced down at his phone when it beeped.

"That was Naya's security detail letting me know they have her in sight and is in route with them." He stated.

She nodded. "Good... I feel a lot better knowing she has people watching and protecting her when we can't."

"Yeah, me too. Let me get out of here so I can handle business and then get back home."

Will pecked her on the lips a few times before he stepped around her and headed for the door. After he left Cori had left a few minutes later to handle some business of her own.

~~~~~~~~~~~~~~~~~~~~~~~~

Inside of Water Tower Place mall, Naya was having a ball. Monica and Alyona had showered her with love, attention, and new shoes and clothes. Whenever Sasha tried to speak to her she would just ignore her. She didn't want to talk to her because she thought she was a mean person.

"Can we go to that store over there? They have earrings and nail polish." Naya pointed across the railing.

"Are you going to polish my nails? I do need a new color." Monica smiled at her.

"Yes, I'll polish your nails, but it won't be for free. A girl got to get paid for her work. At least that's what I heard Katara say before." She looked as if she wasn't sure she had gotten it right.

Alyona giggled. "Yeah, that sounds just like her."

"I wanted to check out this clothing store." Sasha said as she nodded towards the store that was a few feet ahead of them.

"Okay, while you're in there we'll be over at that store. If you finish before us meet us over there. If not we'll meet you back here." Alyona told her.

"Pokhozhe" (I guess) Sasha shrugged and then headed in the store.

Alyona shook her head. "What's her problem?" Monica questioned. She glanced between Alyona and Sasha's back.

"I think she's upset that she's being ignored by a kid. You know she's all about herself and thinks that others should be as well. Being ignored mess with her ego." She whispered for her ears only.

"Oh yeah, I noticed that too. Maybe it would teach her to watch what she says to people." Monica shrugged as they headed inside the store Naya pulled them by the hand to.

Naya's beautiful brown eyes lit up when she saw the different array of fingernail polish, hair bows, bracelets, and everything else a little girl desired. She rushed over to the hair bows and picked a purple one up. She sat it on her head and then turned their way.

"How do I look?"

"You look very pretty." Alyona told her with a smile.

"I would have to agree. I think you should get it along with a few others in different colors."

"Yes!" She jumped up and down. She then turned around and started picking out other hair bows that she liked.

Once they were done picking out hair bows, nail polish, bracelets, and cute little earrings in different shapes they left out the store. Sasha hadn't met them at the store so they headed back to the one she was at. Alyona held on to a happy Naya's hand as they walked through the crowded mall.

Before Alyona could fully understand what was going on, Naya's hand was ripped out of hers. She looked on in horror as a man in all black with a hat covering majority of his face ran with her in his arms. She noticed that Naya didn't scream, fight, or anything. As she ran behind them she noticed the cloth he held over her mouth. When he dropped it Naya's head leaned to the side with her eyes closed like she was sleeping.

"Stop! Help, he's taking her! Naya!" Alyona screamed with tears pouring from her eyes as she ran behind them as fast as should could. Monica was right behind her screaming out for Naya as well.

They then noticed a group of men running pass them at full speed. You would've thought they were at a track meet from how fast they were running. Alyona and Monica started to panic even more because they lost sight of Naya and the man that snatched her.

By the time they made it out of the mall their confusion doubled. One of the men that had ran pass them was walking towards them with Naya in his arms. He handed her over to Alyona. She was still knocked out.

"Get in the car and head straight back to Mr. Cooper's estate." The man told them.

"My other cousin is still in the mall."

"We'll have one of the men go get her home. Now go; a doctor will be there shortly to check her out."

Alyona nodded. "Okay." She and Monica rushed to the car. She knew there would be someone following them to the house so she felt a little better.

The man watched as they got in the car and pulled off. A few seconds later part of the security team pulled off after them.

"The boss is going to be pissed." One of the other guys walked up and said.

"I'm more afraid of how pissed Ms. Romanov is going to be."

"Shit, I didn't think about that. At least we got the guy. Let's get him to one of the warehouses until the boss lets us know what the next move is."

He nodded and they headed to the truck. Inside the trunk was the guy who had snatched Naya. They knew their boss was going to want to question him.

~~~~~~~~~~~~~~~~~~~~~~~~~~~~~~~~

Will watched closely as Zel stepped outside to take a call. He knew it had to be important for him to leave out while he was still in a room with other businessmen. Will was done with the meeting anyway. He said what he had to say and that was it. Nothing else needed to be said.

"Mr. Cooper, I really think you should reconsider my offer." One man by the name of Mattia Cancio said.

"You think so?"

He nodded. "Yes, I do. We could do some great business together."

Will leaned back and smirked. "My problem with that Cancio is that it would only be beneficial to you. When you do business with someone it's supposed to benefit all parties involved. That is why I do not accept your offer."

Zel strolled back in the room and over towards Will. He leaned down by his ear. "We have a serious problem, boss. We need to get out of here and handle it."

"It's that important?"

Zel just nodded in response. Will stood to his feet and fixed his suit jacket.

"Are you leaving so soon?" Mattia asked.

"Yes, this meeting was over anyway. You fellas try to have a good day."

With that he and Zel left out the building. Once they were in the car Will got right to it.

"What's the problem that need my immediate attention?"

"Someone tried to snatch Naya from the mall today."

"What!" He shouted out in anger.

"Our men were able to stop him from leaving with her. She's headed back to the house now. They called the doctor to come and check her out. He had given her something to knock her out."

"What happened to the man that snatched her?"

"Some of the men grabbed him and took him to one of the warehouses."

Will rubbed the top of his head. "Good, take me to the house. I need to check on Naya. He can wait a little longer for his death."

"You got it boss."

Will: Stop whatever you're doing and meet me at the house.

My Heart (Cori): I'm in the middle of a job.

Will: Naya needs you now.

My Heart Cori: I'll be there soon.

He read the message then placed his phone on his lap. He tried hard to keep his anger under control. Inside he was burning with rage. Someone was going to die and soon. Before that happened though, he plan to get the information they've all been seeking.

~~~~~~~~~~~~~~~~~~~~~~~~~~~~~

As soon as Cori rushed through the door she ran right into Will. He stopped her before she was able to get pass him.

"What happened? Where is Naya? Did that bitch Sasha say something to her again? I promise I'm going to snap her damn neck if she did." She sneered.

"Baby, take a deep breath and calm down. Naya is upstairs in her bedroom. She just woke up and she doesn't remember anything."

Cori leaned her head back and looked at him. "What is it that she doesn't remember?"

"Someone tried to snatch her at the mall today."

"What!"

"The guys I had looking after her was able to stop him from taking her. He did however use chloroform to keep her from calling for help. The doctor said that she will be fine, but she doesn't remember being snatched up. The last thing she remembers is shopping with Alyona and Monica."

Cori calmed her breathing down a little. "I need to see her."

Will stepped aside so she could get passed. "We got the guy held up at one of the warehouses. Whenever you're ready to handle that let me know."

She nodded and started to walk towards the stairs then stopped. "Thank you, baby."

"None needed, go see about your sister. I'll be waiting down here for you."

Cori sped to Naya's bedroom. When she got there she saw Alyona and Monica in the room with her. They looked her way when she stepped inside. Alyona stood up and walked up to her.

"Cori, I'm so sorry. I know you trusted me with her and I failed you. I would understand if you never wanted to speak to me again, but please forgive me."

Cori pulled her into a hug. "You have nothing to be sorry about. This isn't a your fault. I don't blame you. I only blame the people involved." She stated and then walked around her over to the small table in the corner of the room.

Naya sat in one of the chairs coloring in her coloring book with Monica. When Monica stood up she followed her eyesight. A huge smile graced her face when she saw her big sister.

"Cori are you going to color with me?"

Cori smiled and sat down. "Sure, princess."

"I had fun at the mall today. I don't remember us leaving though. I think I got tired and fell asleep that's why we left."

196

"I love you, Naya." Cori said as she tried to keep her emotions at bay. It didn't use to be this hard to do. She used to be an emotionless person. That was until she met Will and found Naya. They always made her emotions show whether she wanted them to or not.

"I love you too, Cori."

"Let's call daddy and tell him we love him as well, okay?"

"Okay."

She pulled her phone out and dialed her father's number. He answered the phone on the first ring.

"Hello, sweetheart. I'm in the middle of a mess at the moment."

Cori could hear muffled screams on the other end. "I have Naya here with me and we just wanted to tell you something."

"Hold on one second." Stepan replied.

A few moments later he came back to the phone and his background was completely silent.

"Now what was it you were saying?"

"We love you, papa!" Naya yelled out.

"Yes daddy, we love you very much." Cori told him.

"I love you both more than the air I breathe."

"Naya, I'm going to go out in the hallway and talk to daddy for a minute. You finish coloring with Monica and Alyona." She stood up.

"Okay."

Cori smiled and nodded at Alyona and Monica as she walked passed them out the room. She closed the door behind her.

"What's going on, Cori?" Stepan questioned.

"Someone tried to snatch Naya at the mall today. The team Will has protecting her stopped it from going any farther than the front door. She doesn't remember anything that happened because the guy who snatched her used chloroform on her."

"Are you sure she's okay?"

"Yes a doctor checked her out and everything; she's fine."

"What about the guy that tried to take her?"

"He's held up at a warehouse. I'm heading that way as soon as I get Naya settled."

There was a short pause. "I'll let you handle him. See if it's connected to the other attack. Any information you find out let me know."

"Of course."

"Tell Naya I'm going to FaceTime her on her tablet. I need to see my little girl's face."

"I'll let her know."

"Oh, and Cori..."

"Yes father?"

"Sdelay tak, chtoby etot sukin syn stradal, prezhde chem otpravit' yego v ad." (Make that son of a bitch suffer before you send him to hell.)

Cori smirked. "S udovol'stviyem, papa." (With pleasure, father.)

Alyona and Monica walked out of the bedroom right after she finished the call with her father. They let her know that they were heading home. Sasha kept calling them trying to figure out what was going on. All she knew was that something had happened and one of the security guards had to take her back to Alyona's house. She kept being told that they would explain everything to her later.

Cori said goodbye to them and then headed back in the room with Naya. Will had come upstairs to join them a few minutes later. They spent a few hours with Naya until she went down for bed. Sarah stayed close by her while she slept. Before Will and Cori left the house they made sure it was completely locked down and the guards were on their job.

"No one is getting in there, baby. She's safe in the house." Will assured Cori as they pulled off.

"For the lives of all your men on duty tonight, I hope so." She replied.

Will chuckled and smirked at her threat. He knew she was serious and meant every word. He still found it a little funny how she said it without an ounce of remorse in her tone.

Half an hour later they pulled up to one of the warehouses that Will got located far away from the city. They stepped out of the car and was greeted by Zel. He looked them both up and down.

"You two are dressed like you're about to run down on a bunch of muthafuckas."

Cori smiled as she glanced at their attire. They were both dressed in all black with gun and knife holsters attached to their body. They looked like they were ready for war with whoever wanted a piece of them.

"We might be; we don't know who he was working with yet. They could pop up on us." Cori replied as she led the way inside.

"That would be their biggest fucking mistake." Will said.

"Well, as you can see they're stupid."

Upon entering the building they spotted a man in nothing but his boxers hanging by a hook in the center of the room. The large hook ripped through the middle of both his hand. Blood pour down on him from the wounds. He had a rag tied around his mouth to muffle his screams.

Without warning four knives went into his body. One in each armpit and one in both of his thighs.

"Where the fuck those come from?" One of the guys that was on Naya's security detail asked. It was four of them in the room along with Cori, Will, and Zel.

Cori smirked at how confused they were. They hadn't noticed her pull the knives out or when they left her hands.

"Today boys you're going to see up close what happens when I'm pissed off." She told them.

Cori walked up to where the guy was hanging and stopped a few feet away. "Lower the hook a little."

One of the men lowered it to where he was eye level with her. Cori pulled out a similar knife to the four she threw at him. She dragged it up his chest, but didn't press hard enough to draw blood. She moved up to the rag that covered his mouth and cut it off.

Before he could let out a scream from all the pain he felt she pressed the knife to his lips.

"Shut up all that screaming. You were brave enough to touch my little sister so be brave enough to take the pain." She spat through clenched teeth.

"Now, tell me why you thought it was smart to try and take my sister."

"Please, I'm so sorry. Please!" He cried.

"That's not the answer I was looking for." She took the knife and carved the letter 'D' into his chest. He screamed out from the pain.

"Answer the question!"

"I... I was paid to snatch her."

"By who?"

He ignored that question. "I was supposed to grab her and then hold her until they came for her. I swear I wasn't going to hurt her." He cried.

"Who were you going to hold her for?"

He feverishly shook his head. "I can't... they'll kill me if I tell you."

Cori angrily carved the letters 'E' and 'A' into his chest next to the 'D'. "I always found it funny when people would say that. It's stupid to say when you're staring death right in the face at that very moment." She sneered right before she carved the letters 'T' and 'H'.

She took a step back and admired her handy work. She carved the word DEATH into his chest. It was a puddle of blood beneath him on the floor.

"I'm going to ask you one last time. Who hired you to kidnap her?"

"Please..."

"Are you more afraid of what they're going to do to you than what I am doing right now? Do you not know who I am?"

"I fear you more than them, but you don't kill women and children unless you have to. It doesn't faze them one way or another. I'm willing to die for my children to live."

It was Will's turn to step in. He strolled over and stood beside Cori. "How noble of you? That little speech probably would've helped you just a little bit if it wasn't for the fact you were willing to give Naya to them with no problem. I guess her life wasn't important, huh?" With quick reflexes he pulled his gun out, shot him in both his kneecaps, and then returned his gun to its holster within seconds.

"Ahhhhhhhh!"

Will punched him in the mouth to stop him from screaming. "You didn't care about Naya's life being taken from her. You claim to know who Cori Romanov is and yet you plotted to sentence her sister to death. I guess finding a way to warn her about the attempt on her sister wasn't an option?"

The man spit out blood. He could feel himself about to lose consciousness any minute. "I... I... I'm sorry."

"Tell me who hired you and I might accept your apology." Cori said.

"My... my kids."

Cori sighed. "Here's some hard truth for you. You claim these people are so dangerous and doesn't care about killing kids. You claim that they took your kids in order to get you to work with them against the Romanov family. That tells me one thing; your kids are most likely already dead. They plan to kill you as soon as you delivered Naya. They wouldn't want you leading any trails back to them."

The man started to cry harder. "All you have to do is tell us who it was that hired you and we'll get revenge for your children's deaths as well." Will told him.

"Petrov... the Petrov family hired me to take her. They said that her torture and death would be their revenge for something or someone the Romanovs took from them." He finally confessed.

Cori's eyes blazed with anger. "So, you did know that they would kill her? You're pathetic and your kids are better off without you. You won't be seeing them ever again not even in death. You're going straight to hell."

She took a step back along with Will. Zel stepped up and doused him in gasoline. The guy screamed and cried from the liquid getting into his wounds.

"You should be happy now. Trust me when I say that I'm letting you off easy." When she said that the other men in the room looked at each other. If that was what she called going easy they would hate to see what she does when she goes hard. Will and Zel chuckled at their facial expressions.

"This is light work for her, fellas." Will assured them with a grin on his face.

"Do anybody have a lighter or match? You know what never mind." She pulled her gun out and shot at the floor beneath him. The spark from the bullet ricocheting off the floor where some of the gasoline was caused it to catch on fire. The fire soon spread to the guy's entire body.

Cori watched him burn alive for a few minutes. When his screams started to die down she turned to leave.

"When the fire goes out dispose of what's left of him." Will instructed.

"Hold up, boss. This was on him when we grabbed him." One of the men handed Will a cell phone.

He nodded and followed Cori out of the building and to the car. Once they got inside he pulled off.

"They're going to know that we know when he doesn't call or answer his phone about the drop." She stated in deep thought.

"What do you want to do then?"

"We need to get to Russia as soon as possible."

Will busted a U-turn in the middle of the street. He headed straight for the airport. "Call and tell them to prepare the jet."

Cori pulled her phone out and made the call. She realized that she needed to call her father as well. She would do that once she got on the plane. While making the arrangements for their travel, she could hear Will's phone call too.

"Zel, we're headed to Russia. I want you to watch over Naya until we get back." There was a short pause.

"I'll be fine I can handle myself. Plus, I got my baby by my side. I'll be good, you just make sure Naya stays good."

"Thanks man." He ended the call and focused on the road.

"So, who the hell are the Petrov family?" He asked.

During the drive to the airport Cori explained who they were. By the time they arrived the plane was ready to pull off. Cori made a mental note to call and speak with

Sarah. She wanted to let her know that they'll be gone for a while and to prepare Naya for their absence.

"Back to Russia again." She mumbled to herself.

Chapter 13

Stepan and Alexei had already been waiting for Cori and Will when the plane landed. They greeted one another and jumped right in the truck. Cori had given them every detail of what happened at the warehouse and what was said.

Stepan's entire face was red with anger. "I knew deep down that he could possibly had a hand in it. He sat in our fucking faces and lied!"

"Gervasi must have known that we had someone watching him. That's probably why he hired someone to do it instead of his own family." Alexei stated.

"He's most likely hoping that it doesn't track back to him. That might be why he had the guy's family killed." Will said.

"What is our next move? I'm more on the let's walk through his front door and kill everybody in sight side of things." Cori spat.

"Even though that doesn't sound like a bad idea, we need to think this all the way through. We have to find out if anyone else was involved and who was the person that we supposedly took from them." Alexei said.

Stepan sighed. "Your uncle is right. We need to end this once and for all. First we need to find out who all the players are."

"Whatever we do it has to be done tonight. They're going to know something is up when they don't hear from their guy." Cori told them.

"Well let's get to it then." Alexei stated.

By the time they made it to their destination Stepan and Alexei had already made phone calls to their team. They had all the weapons they would need for their mission ready for them.

Will strolled over to one of the many tables that was scattered throughout the room filled with weapons. He pointed to something and looked back at Cori.

"Is that a damn flame thrower?"

Alexei walked up and patted him on the shoulder. "Yes, would you like to take it?"

"Naw, I'm good on that, but I'll take that rifle machine gun though. I haven't seen one like that before." He walked over and picked it up.

"We just got that in recently."

Cori glanced around the building at all the men preparing for war. She looked over at her father and he was dressed in all black from head to toe.

"You really do look like the Grim Reaper right now."

Stepan chuckled. "Good because I'm about to go collect some souls tonight."

"Listen up! Tonight we show them why they should fear the Romanov name. We show them why they should never go against us! I want a clean sweep tonight boys and lady." He winked at his daughter.

"Just remember that Gervasi Petrov is mine!" He shouted.

Everyone loaded up in the trucks and cars out front. Will sat in the truck beside Cori. She was staring at the side of his face as he examined his guns to make sure they were on point. A smirk spread across his handsome face.

"Why are you staring at me, baby?" He finally looked over at her.

Cori smiled at him. "I'm staring at you because you're mine."

"I'm glad you know that now. It took you a while at first to realize that."

She nodded. "It did, but I'm not that foolish woman anymore."

"Naw, you're not. You're mine though and I'll always ride and protect what's mine."

"I feel the same way."

"Good, so we don't need to have that talk you were about to start. When we get there you can do your thing without worrying about me. I know my way around a gun or two."

"How did you know I..."

He chortled. "I told you a long time ago that we're connected. I know you better than you know yourself now and it's vice versa."

"Just be careful tonight."

Will nodded. "You do the same. Remember that I got plans for us when this is all over."

That caused Cori to smile. She leaned over and kissed his lips. After the kiss she got back into killer mode.

In the truck in front of them Stepan sat beside his brother. "Has the guy we have watching him made any updates yet?" He asked.

"He said that they haven't done anything but sit around drinking and smoking. He also said that there were no women and children in sight."

"That's even better for us. We don't have to worry about them catching a stray bullet."

Alexei nodded in agreement. "From what he says it sounds like they are celebrating. Do you think that's because they feel like they had accomplished something by taking from us? Our mother and now they think that they had gotten Naya."

Stepan thought about the text message he had Will send from the dead guy's phone. He let them believe that he had grabbed Naya and was now holding her. They responded by telling him to hold her for a few days and then someone would come to Chicago to get her. Stepan and Alexei's anger spiked after reading their reply. They didn't understand why Gervasi would be so stupid as to do this.

"Yes, I do believe they're celebrating our loss. No one has ever been able to pull off what they did. They're probably stomping around with their chest buffed out."

"Chto zh, togda tol'ko pravil'no, chto my vydelili im ikh grud' i napomnili im, kto my, chert voz'mi." (Well then it's only right we cave their chest in for them and remind them who the fuck we are.)

"Da, brat, davayte sdelayem eto." (Yes brother, let's do just that.)

~~~~~~~~~~~~~~~~~~~~~~~~~~~~~

Inside of the Petrov estate Gervasi stood around his brothers and cousins smiling. Everything was finally coming together just how he planned it.

"So, what's next cousin?"

"We wait a few days and then send someone to take the little girl. Once we have her, we'll send clues to Stepan on where he can find her. We'll make sure to tell him he has to come with his brother and other daughter."

One of his brothers frowned at that plan. "We're going to reveal our hand in this to them?"

"Not until we have Stepan, Alexei, and Cori Romanov in our sights to take them out."

Some of the men looked around the room at each other. They wasn't so sure about the rest of the plan. They assumed that they would always stay anonymous on what parts they played in all this.

"Are you sure that's a good idea? Stepan and Alexei have men that are very loyal to them. Even if we were to succeed with killing the three of them they would hunt for their killers until their last breaths." Another one of his cousins stated.

"Let's also not forget the man that Cori is with. He has a mean reputation of his own. He was considered a son to Julian before he died. Julian had trained him well and he's not a force to be reckoned with. I doubt that he would let her death go unanswered." His brother said.

Gervasi stared at them. "What do you all suppose we do then?"

"Well for starters you all probably should've had this conversation before you decided to fuck with my family. That's just my opinion though." Alexei appeared from out of the shadows.

Each man's eyes widened with shock. Some went for their weapons, but stopped when they realized that they didn't have any on them. They didn't think that they needed them since they were surrounded by family and had guards watching the house.

"Don't worry about the guards you had surrounding the outside and inside of the house. They're all dead already." Stepan said as he walked into the room followed by Cori. Will had just let them know he killed the last of the guards.

"Stepan, I would think about this before you do anything." Gervasi said in a shaky voice.

"You would? I find that hard to believe since you didn't even think this plan all the way through."

"I can get you back your daughter." He tried to reason with him.

"I don't need your help with that. I know exactly where my daughter is. I have one standing beside me ready to skin you and your entire family in this room alive. I have another one who is mostly likely having a healthy breakfast in Chicago right now. That's if she didn't talk her nanny into giving her donuts for breakfast. She loves those sugary things." Stepan glared at him in the face and then laughed.

"Oh, did you really think you were going to succeed at taken my daughter? Shame on you for being so stupid."

"I'm sorry!"

"Was that before or after your men killed my grandmother?" Cori questioned as she shot his brother in the head. She didn't even look his way when she did it. Her eyes stayed trained on Gervasi.

"I didn't kill your grandmother, I swear!"

Alexei shot one of his cousins right between the eyes. "Of course you didn't. You were too pussy to do it yourself. You had your men do it for you."

"No, no, no, please!"

Stepan shot two of his cousins in the head with one bullet. It had went through one of their head and came out the other.

"Impressive old man." Cori smirked.

"You're only as old as you act and I'm far from old, baby girl."

"I didn't even want to go through with this plan! I told him that it was stupid from the start!" Gervasi's other brother and the only one left alive besides him yelled out.

"Yet, you still went along with it." Alexei sneered.

"He's my family and he said that we were doing it to revenge our blood that you all had taken from us."

"Who?" Cori and Stepan both spoke at the same time.

"Tell them!" He yelled at Gervasi.

"I had gotten word that you all were the cause of our cousin's death. It was marked an accident, but we were told that you all made it look that way. You had injected him with something that couldn't be detected on a blood test. That car crash wasn't an accident it was murder!"

Stepan and Alexei glanced at each other and then back at them. "You think that we killed Adrian?" Stepan questioned.

"What reason would we have to kill him for?" Alexei asked.

"You believe that he's the reason for your sister's disappearance. You think that he murdered his wife so you killed him for it. You couldn't accept that your sister was a whore and probably just ran off with another Italian lover!" Gervasi.

The room was silent for a moment until Stepan, Cori, and Alexei all laughed. The other two men in the room looked confused. They couldn't understand why they were laughing at what was said.

"We didn't think Adrian did anything to our sister." Alexei chuckled.

"Then why did you kill him?"

"We didn't kill him so you got your information mixed up. We're not blaming anyone for Elise's disappearance. We know exactly where she's at."

"You do?"

Stepan nodded. "She's dead and I'm the one who pulled the trigger."

"So, in other words you did all of this for nothing. You're going to die for nothing." Cori said and then shot his brother directly in the face.

"Wait, we can work something out!" Gervasi shouted but his voice was silenced by the bullet Stepan sent through his mouth. The bullet came out the back of his head and spray painted the wall behind him.

"Burn the house down to the ground. I want the message to be loud and clear. Going against a Romanov is punished by death." Stepan glanced at Cori.

"It's time my baby comes home."

She nodded and followed him out of the house. When she got back in the car with Will she noticed him cleaning the rifle machine gun.

"You're going to keep that aren't you?"

He smirked. "Hell yeah!"

She threw her head back and laughed. He stared at her for a moment. "Y'all had gotten everything squared away?"

"Yes and now we can go back home."

"Tomorrow; we'll leave tomorrow. I need to speak with your father about something."

Cori looked at him and then nodded. "Okay." She leaned into him and rested her head on his shoulder.

Later that night while Cori was resting, Will met up with Stepan and Alexei in his office. As soon as he walked in he was handed a drink.

"I'm sure you need one of these as much as we do. I want to thank you for riding this out with us." Stepan patted him on the back.

"I love your daughter and she's considered my family so that makes y'all my family too." He replied.

"Well in that case thank you loving my daughter then."

"I was hoping for more of a blessing than a thanks." Will stared him in the eyes.

"What do you mean?"

"I want to marry Cori and since you're her father I'm asking you for her hand in marriage."

Stepan smiled at him. "I had waited for this day to come. I knew when I first saw the way you looked at my daughter that you were the one for her. She was stubborn for a minute, but she eventually got it together."

"I gave her little mean ass no choice." Will said causing them all to laugh.

"Will, I would be honored to have you as my son-in-law. I give you my full blessing even though I doubt you really needed it. I like the gesture though and I respect you even more for it."

"Yes! Now let's drink to this!" Alexei handed both men a shot glass filled with the best vodka.

"To family!" He held out his glass. Will and Stepan did the same.

"Sem'ye!" (Family!) All three men shouted before they swallowed the shot down with one big gulp.

~~~~~~~~~~~~~~~~~~~~~~~~~~~~~~~~

The following night Will decided to take Cori on a romantic dinner before they had to head back to Chicago. Cori was all for it because she loved spending quality time with her man. He helped balance out her life.

"This place is nice, babe. The food was delicious too. I've never been here before or even knew this place existed." She said as she glanced around the dimly lit restaurant. They had just finished having dinner and was now working on dessert.

"Your father told me about this place. He said that he used to bring your mother here. It was her favorite restaurant."

Cori placed her attention back on him. "Really? He never mentioned that to me."

"It might be a soft spot for him. The only reason he recommended it to me was because I told him I wanted to take you somewhere special. He said that this place would be perfect."

"He was right it is perfect."

"You remember when I told you that after all that shit was over and done with that I had plans for us?"

"Yes."

"I think now is the perfect time I share some of those plans with you." He stood up from his seat and got down on one knee in front of her. He pulled out a small burgundy box from his pocket. Cori looked shocked and happy at the same time.

"Cori, the first time I saw you I couldn't keep my eyes off of you. It wasn't because of the way your body looked in that skin tight jumpsuit you wore either." They both chuckled.

"It was just something about your aura that kept pulling me to you. After we got to know each other I fell head over heels in love with you. You're my best friend, lover, and confidant. I now ask one more title of you. Would you do me the honor of becoming my wife? Will you marry me, baby?"

"Yes!" She shouted out not caring about any of the other patrons in the restaurant.

Will opened the box and pulled the huge diamond ring out. He slid it on her finger and then stood up pulling her into his arms. They shared a passionate kiss while the other patrons clapped and congratulated them.

"Let's go home, baby." He pecked her on the lips a few more times before he paid the bill and then pulled her by the hand to the car.

"Is this what you wanted to talk to my father about?" Cori asked as they headed to the airstrip where the plane was waiting.

"Yes, I asked him for his blessing. He gave it with no problem. He actually said that he had been waiting on it."

"I love you, Will." She leaned over and kissed his cheek.

"I love you too, baby. You do know when we get on this plane I'm about to tear that pussy up right."

Cori laughed. "Promises, promises Mr. Cooper."

"Oh okay, we'll see in a minute if I keep my promises."

She smiled to herself because she knew that she was about to get the best fuck of her life in the sky. If it was one thing he did, he always kept his promises.

Chapter 14

A month had flown by like a breeze in the spring time. Things had been going well for everyone. They had gotten back into their regular routines. Naya had went home a few days after Cori and Will gotten back from Russia. She was back in Chicago with them again for Fall break. Even though she was homeschool Stepan still made sure she got breaks like the other kids.

Katara, Heidi, and Alyona decided to throw Cori and Will an engagement party. It would mostly be family since both didn't really do many friends. The girls were fine with that. They had gotten everyone who meant something to Will and Cori together to help them celebrate.

"I can't believe y'all put this together so quickly." Cori said as she glanced around the beautiful decorated venue.

"We got the magic touch." Katara told her.

"Oh and Will's credit card." Heidi said causing them all to laugh.

"So, basically we paid for our own engagement party?"

Heidi waved her off. "We don't pay attention to the details."

"Thank you guys anyway for doing this for us. We both love it."

"Aww you're welcome, bestie." Katara gave her a hug. She spotted Zel off in the corner and excused her before heading his way.

"Those two have really gotten close over the last few weeks." Cori commented.

"Yes, she's so happy lately and I hope it continues to stay that way."

"I do too she deserves to be happy."

Katara walked up on Zel and tapped him on the shoulder. He turned to face her with a smile on his face.

"Hey beautiful." He greeted her.

"Hi, are you enjoying the party?"

"If I wasn't I sure am now."

She blushed. "You always have a way with words that makes a woman feel good."

"I do and I have a way with other things as well. You know that from experience." He licked his lips and smirked.

Katara giggled. "You are a mess."

Zel chuckled. "Tell that to my sheets you messed up the other night."

She covered her face to try and hide her smile. Flashes of what he did to her body the other night ran through her mind. Her body started to react to the memory. She had to squeeze her thighs together to ease the throbbing between her legs.

He pulled her hands away from her face. "Stop trying to hide that beautiful face from me. You know how much I love looking in your eyes."

"Where is Zela?" She asked trying to change the subject.

He knew what she was doing and let it slide for now. "She wanted to come, but her mom swore that she had plans for her already. I don't even want to get into all that because all it would do is piss me off."

Katara nodded. They had talked a few times about his situation with his daughter's mother. She didn't really give an opinion on the situation because it wasn't her business. She's new to his life and didn't want to overstep her boundaries. Katara did however let him vent when he needed to. She loved the way he love his daughter. The little girl was his world and she felt sad whenever Zela cried when she had to leave her daddy. A true daddy's girl Katara thought when she saw them together. Katara was happy that Zela wasn't spoiled and she was very respectful. She was truly feeling Zel and could see their relationship blossoming into something beautiful.

"I want to take you on another date tomorrow night." He said getting her attention again.

"What kind of date?"

"Just a chill relaxing date. I enjoy spending time with you, Katara."

She smiled up at him. "I enjoy spending with you too. I would love to go on another date with you."

He pulled her to him by the waist. "We're going to make this thing with us work. I know our schedules be interfering with our time, but you make time for what you want. I want you and I'm willing to put in the work to show you that." He told her.

"Where have you been all my life?" She asked and he laughed. She didn't crack a smile because she was serious. Katara had been looking for real love and companionship for years. Never had she had a man treat her the way that Zel did. It was still early in their relationship, but he was starting off good.

"I was probably wasting my time with someone who didn't deserve it." He responded.

She pulled his face down towards hers and kissed his lips. "That makes both of us, but now things are different."

He smirked at her. "It's much different, beautiful."

While Zel and Katara talk and laugh with each other like they've known each other for years; Alyona sat across the room with Sasha. She noticed how Sasha kept looking around like she didn't want to be there. Her attitude was starting to irk Alyona. She finally decided to speak on it, but before she could Sasha started in with her snide little comments again.

"I didn't know people like her really fall in love. I wonder if she's putting on a show and just doing this for uncle Stepan."

Alyona glared at her. "Okay, that's it. I tried to be the peace maker in the situation, but you are truly unbearable. What is your problem with Cori? I want the truth, Sasha."

Sasha rolled her eyes. "Come on Alyona, stop acting like you never noticed how everyone treated her different than the rest of us. Grandmother used to always act like Cori was so special. She was her favorite and it wasn't right."

"Are you serious right now?"

"Yes, I am."

"Sasha, grandma never picked favorites between us. It may have seemed that way, but it's not true. She basically helped raise Cori."

"It wasn't our fault that she didn't have a mother and we did."

Alyona reached out and slapped her so hard that her hand print was left on the side of her face. Sasha held her cheek as she glared at Alyona in shock. Lucky for her no one had paid them any attention.

"You are a horrible person to say such a thing about our cousin. She is our family; our blood and you are acting childish. You're jealous of her Sasha. It shows clearly whenever you are around her. Cori never did anything to you that would make you hate her so much. I think that you should pack up your things and leave."

"Alyona..."

She raised her hand to stop her from speaking. "You need to go work on yourself because your heart is rotten." She got up and walked away.

Tears sat at the brim of Sasha's eyes as she watched her walk away. She then stood up and left the party. It was time she headed back home to Russia. Chicago wasn't the place for her at all.

~~~~~~~~~~~~~~~~~~~~~~~~~~~~~

After the party Will and Cori sat in their home theater watching a movie with Naya. She was already falling asleep and the movie was only a few minutes in. Cori and Will looked at her and laughed while she tried to fight her sleep.

Cori glanced at Will. "I'm going to take her upstairs and put her in the bed. I'll be right back."

"Do you need any help?"

She shook her head as she lifted Naya up in her arms. "No, I got it. I'll be back soon."

"Okay, I got a phone call I need to make anyway."

"To the friend that called you for some help?"

"Yeah."

"Okay."

Once Cori left Will pulled his phone out and was about to make a call. He paused when he noticed the incoming call.

"Damn, you must be a physic. I was just about to call you." Will said into the phone.

"Man, I don't mean to keep calling you, but shit is getting bad on my end." Kasim said stressed.

"You already know it's not a problem. I would've been and got back at you, but I got busy over this way. Anyway, I got that information you needed."

"Talk to me then."

"The man behind the threats being sent you and your sister-in-law's way is named Nate Woods. He went from being a petty thief to extorting money and other things from rich business owners. He's made a big name for himself in the criminal world. Lately, he's been heavy into stolen art pieces, counterfeits, and drugs."

"Damn, so that's how he came across me and Zanni?"

"I don't know, but he's been doing business with a few other shady characters lately. My tech guy said that he's been communicating a lot with some art dude named Prestige and a dude out in China by the name of Jason. His father owns a few businesses out in St. Louis and he's also into politics." Will stated as he rubbed his chin.

"You got to be fucking kidding me?"

"Yeah, I thought you'll see the connection now too. Both those dudes knew your sister-in-law. One of them I think she did business with and the other one she was once engaged to. I don't know what she did to piss them off, but they're trying hard to take her down." He said.

"I'm trying to figure out how the hell they know each other."

"They probably met out in China. The Prestige dude had a few art shows out there within the last year. The Jason dude lives and does business out there for his father."

"Okay, I do remember things not ending well with both of them when it came to Zanni. She broke up with the Jason dude and she refused to ever work with that Prestige dude again after what happened between him, my sister, and her husband." Kasim thought about it for a minute.

"That explains a little on why they coming for her, but why you?"

"Prestige is probably coming at me because he can't get to my sister. I wasn't too friendly with that nigga when I saw him."

"Well, it looks like they got with Nate to try and set y'all up. If y'all get caught during the shit he wants y'all to do, not only will your business be shut down, but you'll be looking at a long jail sentence."

"Yeah, you're right about that. Look, thanks for getting this information for me, Will." Kasim said.

"Man, it's not a problem. Just because you're not in the business anymore doesn't mean we're not boys. If you need help with handling this let me know. It's ways to get it taken care of without getting your hands dirty."

"I might have to take you up on that offer. I'm not the old Kasim anymore. I got a family to think about now."

"Yeah, I know man."

"Speaking of family, congratulations on the engagement. I knew when you told me about Cori, she was the one."

Will chuckled. "That's my baby...but yeah let me know if you need my help. I know the perfect person that can have that handled for you without any issues."

"Let me run it by them first and I'll get back at you. Are you back in Chicago or still out in Russia?" Kasim asked him.

"Naw, I'm back home now. Russia kept me busy though." Will said without going into more detail.

"I bet... thanks again man, I appreciate it."

"None needed, handle your business." He said before he ended the call.

Will stared up at the movie screen as he waited for Cori to return. A few minutes later he got a text from Kasim.

Kasim: That help you spoke of could be useful to us.

Will: Done. I'll hit you with the details tomorrow.

Kasim: Cool... thanks again.

He put his phone down right when Cori strolled back in the room. She had changed into her black silk robe.

"I was wondering what was taking you so long."

She smiled at him. "I decided to change into something more comfortable."

He bit down on his bottom lip. "I can see that."

Cori sat on his lap. She leaned forward and gave him a passionate kiss. His hands found their way sliding under her robe. She grinned inside when he realized that she was naked underneath.

"Oh, you're trying to get fucked, huh?"

"That was the plan." She pulled his shirt over his head and then tossed it on the seat beside them.

He kissed her neck. "I have a job for you."

She looked him in the eyes. "Play now, work later."

"You got it, baby."

Will watched as she pulled his dick out of his boxer briefs and sweatpants. He stared as her hands slid up and down his length.

"You're being a tease, baby."

"I'm sorry, what should I do with this big pole again?"

He smirked. "You never needed help with handling it before. Are you trying to tell me something?"

She shook her head. "Nope." She lifted up and then slid down his dick. She held on to his shoulders to keep herself balanced. A moan escaped her lips from the feeling of him being deep inside her.

Will gripped her ass cheeks and pushed into her. She started to twirl and bounce in his lap. He used one hand to open her robe. Her nice round perfect light caramel breast stared him in the face. He took that time to suck on her nipples.

"Will!" She started to bounce faster on him.

"What do you need from me, baby?" He asked as he flicked his tongue across her nipple.

"I need... I need..."

"You need what? Closed mouths don't get fed. Tell me what you want from me." He slapped her on the ass.

"I want you to make me cum!" She moaned out.

"You want to cum or you need to cum? Which one is it, beautiful?"

Cori could feel her orgasm about to hit. She moved faster and faster to reach her peak. "I need to cum!"

He licked her chin and then kissed her lips. "I'm not stopping you, sexy. You know how to get what you want; now take it." He pounded into her harder and faster.

"Oooh Will... Ooooh yes!"

"Come on baby, take what's yours."

"Oooh, it's mine!"

"Yes, now take it."

"Ooooh! Mine!" Her body shuddered as she came harder than she's ever came before.

Will smirked as he came right behind her. He love watching her faces when she's getting fucked.

Cori put her head down on his shoulder as she tried to catch her breath. When she got her breathing under control she leaned up and looked at him.

"Now, you said you had a job for me?"

Will stared at her for a moment and started laughing. "Your legs still shaking, you barely breathing properly, and you're asking about work right now?"

Cori grinned. "I told you play now and work later. It's now later, baby."

He shook his head with a smirk on his face. He stood up with her still in his arms and him still buried deep inside her.

"Let's go take a shower and then we'll talk business."

She wrapped her arms around his neck and kissed him again. "Can we play a little more in the shower?"

"We can do whatever your little heart desires."

Will walked them into the bathroom that was connected to the movie theater room. He knew by the time they got out the shower Cori would be too tired to talk about anything. They'll most likely discuss business in the morning.

"I love you, Mr. Cooper."

"I love you too, soon to be Mrs. Cooper." He said before he kissed her on the neck.

Chapter 15

~A few days later~

Cari had gone to New York on business leaving Will and Naya to spend some time together. Naya was all too excited to spend time with Will. They had gone to the pizzeria and kid's spa. She was having a blast.

"Naya, how would you like to come visit my parents with me?" He glanced at her in the back seat through the mirror.

"I would love to."

"Okay, so let me give you a few tips about them."

"Okay."

"They are my adoptive parents."

"You're adopted too?" She asked shocked.

"Yes, they were already my godparents, but they adopted me when I was fifteen. To me they are the only parents I know and I love them."

"I can't wait to meet them. Why weren't they at the party?"

"They were on vacation at the time and just got back yesterday."

"Oh."

A few minutes later they pulled up to a nice three story brick house. Naya smiled at the pretty flowers in the garden.

Will got out and then helped Naya out of her booster seat. Before they could knock on the door it came open.

"What's up, Pops?"

"You finally decided to stop by, huh? I guess your mother's threats was starting to get to you."

Will chuckled and then shook his head. "You know she has a way with words and her hands."

They shared a laugh and then Nico looked down at Naya. "Is this the pretty little girl that you and Cori talk about?"

"Yeah, this is Naya, Cori's little sister. Naya, this is my Pops Nico."

"Hi, Mr. Nico." She waved up at him.

"Hello pretty girl, you can just call me Nico."

"Okay."

"Y'all come on in here. Your mother in the kitchen. When you done talking to her let me speak with you about something."

"From the look on your face it must be serious."

"You can say that."

He nodded and then led Naya into the kitchen to see his mother. When they stepped into the room they saw Adele in there moving around the kitchen cooking.

"You always got it in here smelling good." Will said getting her attention.

Adele turned around and smiled at the sight of her son's face. "Boy, get over here and give me a hug."

He did as he was told and kissed her on the cheek. "You look beautiful as always."

"Will, stop trying to sweet talk me. Did you talk to your father yet?"

That question caused him to frown a little. "No, not yet but it must be something real important since y'all both mentioning it."

"Just go in there and talk to him. Keep an open mind about things when you do."

"Ma, that's not sounding good. Are y'all two okay?"

"Yes, we're fine just talk to your father."

He stared at her for a moment and then nodded. "Okay, I'll talk to him but first I want you to meet Naya."

Adele smiled at the pretty little girl that stood next to Will. "Is this Cori's little sister? She showed me pictures of her, but they don't do her any justice. She is beautiful."

Naya blushed. "Thank you, my name is Naya."

"Hello little Ms. Naya. My name is Adele, but you can call me nana if you want to."

"Really?"

"You sure can. I was just about to start on dessert. Would you like to help me make it?"

Naya looked up at Will. "Can I help, please?"

"Yeah, go ahead."

Adele looked at him and waved him off. "You can go talk to your father while we're cooking."

He chuckled and left out the kitchen. He found his father seated in the living room in his favorite chair.

"What are you in here watching, Pops?"

"I'm just going over some of the kid's old plays." Nico sat up straight and paused the television.

"What's going on, Pops? You and mom got me worried."

"I had ran into Gary the other day while I was out running errands for your mama." Nico started.

Will twisted his face up at the mention of his biological dad. He didn't understand why his father was telling him about Gary. He had no love or care in the world for that man.

"I don't care about him."

"Will, Gary is dying and..."

"I still don't care, Pops. That dude doesn't mean anything to me."

"I think you should go meet up with him and talk to him."

"Why, because he's dying? I don't care about him dying, Pops. In my opinion it took too long for him to die anyway. He should've been died."

"No, not because he's dying but because he has some information that he needs to tell you."

"Why couldn't he had just told you so you can tell me? I don't want to talk to him about anything."

Nico rested his elbows on his knees and looked his son square in the eyes. "Now, you know any other time I wouldn't give a damn about him either. I'm telling you this because I think he knows something that you really need to hear, Will. Just go talk to him and then after that you don't have to worry about ever speaking to him again. From the way he looked he'll be dead soon anyway."

He thought about it for a moment. "I'll think about it. That's all I can do at the moment, Pops."

Nico nodded. "That's better than nothing."

They sat in the living room and watched television until Adele called them in the kitchen to eat. Will and Naya had dinner with his parents and then headed back home. The entire time he thought about what his Pops told him. He made a decision to go have a chat with Gary soon. He wasn't sure what would come from it, but he was willing to do it more so for his parents. They thought it was important that he talk to him so for them he'll do it.

~~~~~~~~~~~~~~~~~~~~~~~~~~~

Out in New York Cori was doing what she do best. Dressed in a housekeeper uniform she rolled the cart down the hotel's hallway. She passed a man in the hallway and recognized him as one of her targets.

"I'll be seeing you soon too, Mr. Nate." She thought.

When she found the room number that she was looking for, she knocked on the door.

"Housekeeping!" She yelled through the door.

"Do we need anything from housekeeping?" She heard a man ask someone else that was inside the room with him.

"Yes, I need new sheets on my bed and a few more towels. I had called down there over thirty minutes ago though." Another man replied.

"Oh okay." The door opened up and the man allowed her inside the room. Once she was all the way in he closed the door behind her.

"Hello, I'm your housekeeper..."

"It's about time somebody showed up. I called down there thirty minutes ago." The other man that stood a few feet away stated.

"He must be the Jason guy." She thought.

"Oh sorry, the shift had changed and I didn't get notified about it until recently."

"I need the bed made with new sheets and some more towels." Jason told her.

"Sure, I'll get right to it." Cori nodded.

"I hope I don't offend you when I ask this, but what is your nationality?" The first guy who she knew to be Prestige asked as he eyed her. Cori knew that she was a very beautiful and attractive woman. She also learned that he was more of the wannabe player of the two men.

She shook her head. "No, I don't mind at all. I'm actually mixed..."

"With what?" He asked cutting her off.

"My mother is African American and my father is Russian."

"Oh okay... I'm sorry if I'm coming off rude, but you are very beautiful."

"Thank you." She grabbed some clean sheets off the cart.

"What is your name, beautiful?"

"Cori..."

"That's a man's name." Jason said with his face twisted up.

She glared at him. "It's actually an unisex name. Meaning that it could be used for a boy or a girl name."

"I think it's a nice name." Prestige smiled at her.

She returned his smile. "Thank you. Now which room need the new sheets?" She asked.

"Follow me I'll show you." Jason turned and led her to his room. He refused to let her in there without being able to watch her. He heard about housekeepers stealing from guest all the time.

"Here it is and can you make this quick?" He pointed to the bed once they walked in the room.

"I was actually going to take my time with this, but you are so annoying." She said.

"Excuse me?"

"Oh now you got manners? Anyway, Zaniela sends her regards on not being able to be here and watch you take your last breath." She shook her head and pulled her gun out with the silencer on it.

"What?" Jason looked at her confused. When he saw the gun he was going to scream, but the bullet she sent straight through his mouth stopped all of that. The bullet flew out the back of his head with a lot of his blood and brain matter. His body dropped to the floor with a loud thud.

"Is everything okay in here?" Prestige questioned as he walked to the door. His eyes widened at the sight of Jason laid out on the floor on his stomach with a huge hole in the back of his head. He then glanced at the housekeeper Cori and found her staring at him with a smirk on her face.

He turned around and was about to make a run for it until she shot him in the back of the leg. He instantly dropped to the floor. When he started crawling she walked up and shot him in the other leg.

"Ahhhhhhhh! Why are you doing this? Please don't kill me." He cried out.

"Well, if it wasn't for you and your friend back there I wouldn't be here right now." She kicked him over onto his back.

"Wha... what are talking about?"

"Kasim Davis and Zaniela Brennan ring any bells?"

His eyes widened like they did when he saw Jason's dead body. "I figured that they would since you and your friend in there hired someone to ruin their lives. That's okay, I'm here to make sure that doesn't happen." She lifted the hand up with the gun in it and aimed it at his forehead.

"I'll double whatever they're paying you!" He yelled out.

"As nice as that sounds, you can't afford me. Plus, they're considered family and friends to my fiancé. I don't want to start our marriage off on bad terms, you know? Of course you don't because you're stupid." She said and then sent two bullets into his skull. She pulled out a phone and snapped a picture of him and did the same with the other guy.

"Two down and one to go." Cori said as she walked over to her cart. She made sure she didn't get any blood on her. Once she saw that she was good to go she opened the door and pushed her cart out. She place a 'Do Not Disturb' sign on the door and walked off whistling as she pushed the cart down the hallway towards the elevators.

Cori had made it to her next destination in record timing. She wasn't surprised that it was another cheap hotel. This time she wasn't dressed like a housekeeper. Instead she wore jeans, a leather jacket, and leather high heel boots.

As she made her way off the elevator a woman dressed in revealing clothes rushed pass her on to it. The lady looked like she was running from someone. She found out that her thought were correct when she saw a naked man run pass her towards the elevators. Cori smiled as she realized that the man was her next target. While he beat on the closed elevator doors, she slipped into his hotel room.

"I'm going to find and kill that bitch. It can't be that many prostitutes by the name Rose Mills." Nate spat as he slammed the hotel door shut.

He stormed inside the room and headed straight for the mini bar. "Are you having a rough night?" Cori questioned from over in the corner of the room.

Nate swung around in the direction he heard the voice come from. He noticed it was the housekeeper from the other hotel. Her hair was now a different color. Back at the other hotel it was blonde, but now she's a brunette with curls.

"How did you get in here?" He asked with a confused facial expression plastered on his face.

"Oh, I just walked right in while you were chasing after your little lady friend." She smirked.

"What are you doing here?"

"You ask a lot of questions, you know that?"

"Do you work at this hotel too?" He asked still not understanding what she was doing there in his hotel room.

Cori sighed. "None of you are that bright. For someone who's trying to destroy somebody else's life, you all are dumb."

"What the hell are you talking about?"

"I don't have time for this at all. I could be back home with my man practicing on going half on some babies. Kasim and Zaniela says fuck you and rot in hell."

"Wait!"

It was too late for any of that. Cori had already sent four shots to his body; two to the head and Two to the heart. He was dead before his body hit the floor. She snapped a picture of him like she had done the others.

Cori strolled out of the room and out of the hotel as if nothing happened. Once she got in her rental car and pulled off, she dialed a number on her phone.

"Are you done already, baby?" Will asked from the other end of the phone.

"Yes, it's all done and I'll be sending you the pictures so that you could send it to them."

"Okay good, now bring your fine ass home."

Cori smiled. "I'm headed to the airport now, baby."

"I'll see you soon then."

"Yes, you will and I hope you're not too busy for me when I get there."

He laughed. "I'm never too busy for you, beautiful. I love you."

"I love you too, Will."

"Now hurry up, I miss you."

Cori had a smile on her face the entire ride to the airport.

~~~~~~~~~~~~~~~~~~~~~~~~~~~~

The following few days Cori relaxed with her man. Her father had come into town to pick up Naya, but she wasn't ready to go home. Stepan decided to go stay a few days so she could stay and play with her friend Zela a little longer. When it was time to leave and go home again this time she did so without fussing.

Will and Cori had finally had the house to themselves again. They celebrated by sexing each other all over the house. During one of their late night talks they discussed the situation with Gary. Will had yet to go see him and Cori agreed with his parents. She told him that he should go talk to him.

That was the only reason Will stood in front of the house that he spent miserable years in growing up. The house now looked like it was about to fall apart any minute. He dragged his hand down his face and walked up to the door. He knocked on it twice and then waited. When no one answered the door he knocked again, but this time harder.

"Are you looking for Gary?" He heard someone say from behind him.

Will turned around and saw an old lady standing by the gate. He walked down the steps and over to where she stood.

"Yeah, I'm looking for him."

"They had took him to the hospital the other day. He was real sick. It's most likely from all that damn alcohol he drinks. His damn liver and lungs giving out on him now. Serves him right for how he used to treat his wife back in the day." She stated with a roll of her eyes.

"What hospital did they take him to?"

"I believe it was Barnes."

"Thank you."

"Oh, you're welcome baby. Tell the old fucker I said hey if he ain't already dead." She said and then walked back next door to her house.

Will shook his head and jumped back in his car. He drove to the hospital and asked the front desk nurse for Gary's room. He was almost disappointed when she gave him one. He was low key hoping that he had passed away already so he wouldn't have to talk to him.

When he got to the room a nurse was walking out. He stopped her for a minute. "How is he doing?"

"Are you some kin to Mr. Cooper?"

"I guess you can say that. He donating sperm to help produce me."

She stared at him for a second and then looked around. "Mr. Cooper is dying and the doctor said that he might not even make it overnight."

"Thanks."

"You're welcome."

Will walked in the room and saw that Gary was awake. He looked like a shadow of the guy he used to be. His skin was ashy and his eyes were sunk in.

Gary saw Will walk in and pushed the button for the bed to lift up some. "I was hoping that Nico was able to get you to come." He coughed out.

Will stood a few feet away from the bed with his hands buried in his pockets. "What did you want to talk with me about?"

"I'm not going to beat around the bush with you. I don't have time to anyway. When your mama was pregnant with you I was cheating on her with a younger woman. Her name was Patrice. She made me feel young again and I felt your mama was draining my youth. Anyway, after your mama gave birth to you Patrice had told me that she was pregnant. I felt bad about cheating on your mama so I broke things off with Patrice and told her to get an abortion. I told her that I was going to work on my family and I didn't need an outside baby messing that up. Months later she got word to me that she gave birth to a baby boy. Again, I didn't want to mess up my family so I told her that I didn't want anything to do with her or the baby."

Will stood there listening to him in shock. "Are you telling me that I got a little brother out there somewhere?"

Gary nodded and started to cough. "Yes. I don't know his name or where he's at though. I do know that Patrice wasn't from Chicago. She was from St. Louis I think. That's all I know. I thought that it was right that I tell you."

He scoffed. "You waited until you were on your death bed to tell me that I had a damn brother. I already knew you weren't shit Gary, but this is fucking low of you. You disown your own child, for what? You still treated your wife like shit."

"I know..."

"Was this all you needed to tell me? I don't have any other siblings out there do I?"

"No, I'm sorry for all the pain I caused you."

"I'm not the one you need to be apologizing to. She's already gone and I'm sure the son you disowned wouldn't give a fuck now. I hope you asked the big guy up there for forgiveness because he's the only one that can help you." Will stated and then walked out of the room and straight out of the hospital. He couldn't believe the information that Gary just laid out on him.

"A brother..." He mumbled as he jumped in his car and pull off.

He made a mental note to hire a private investigator to find his brother. Gary didn't give much to go on, but it would have to do.

"I have a fucking brother." He said out loud still in disbelief.

A few days after Will visited Gary at the hospital he died of alcohol poisoning and liver failure. Will didn't feel anyway about it. Gary was never a father to him. He couldn't find anything in him to care about him.

Will had since then contacted a private investigator to help him find his brother. He gave him all the information that Gary gave him. It wasn't much, but he said that he would do his best. Now it was just the waiting game.

Meanwhile, Will had gotten a phone call from an old friend asking for a favor. His people were looking for a new connect and he thought about him. He agreed to meet with his people and go from there. Will liked Malik, but he had to be careful with who he did business with. Malik understood and said that he would pass his information along.

Now Will sat in his office at one of his buildings waiting for the guy to arrive. He watched the monitors as a car pulled up outside. He stayed put to see how the person would handle his security team. A smiled cracked his face as he watched and listen to the man go back and forth with Jesse. One of the newer guys on the team. The man was refusing to give up his weapons. Will then watched as Zel made his way over towards them.

Jesse took a step towards the dude, but stopped when he heard his name being called out.

"Jesse, it's cool let him pass!"

Jesse stepped to the side but glared at the guy as he walked passed.

"That would've been an easy bet." The dude smirked at Jesse.

"Jesse just doing his job don't let him get to you."

"I wasn't tripping off him. Like I said I wasn't come up off my shit." He said.

Zel chuckled and looked back at him over his shoulder. "You and my boss should get along just fine. Follow me to the back."

They walked all the way to the back of the warehouse. When they got to a metal door they stopped. The dude watched as Zel pressed a button and then glanced up at the camera above the door. A few seconds later the door opened up.

"Thanks Zel, I can handle it from here." Will said from inside the room.

"Sure thing boss."

The dude strolled into the room and the door closed behind him. He looked at Will who sat on the front edge of the desk. Will looked familiar and he was trying to place where he may have known him from. Will stared right back at him during the same.

"You are one of Malik's friends." Will said more as a statement than a question. He answered anyway.

"Yeah..."

"Well, if Malik trust you than you're cool with me until you're not. I'm Will and you must be Pete, right?"

"Yeah, it's just me and my boy Zyir."

"I know... I'm good with remembering faces and I don't think we've met before but you look familiar." Will said with a confused look on his face.

"I was thinking the same thing."

"Well, do you have any questions before you meet the connect?" Will asked him.

Pete was a little shocked, but he didn't let his face show it. "I didn't know I was meeting the connect today. I thought you wanted to meet up first to feel us out."

"That was the original plan, but things changed. Like I said Malik is a good friend of mine. We did a lot of business together. He trust you and your boy Zyir. Plus, I did my own research on y'all myself. Y'all about y'all business just like me. I can respect a man that gets out here and handle his business."

"So, you're going to get us in good with your connect?" Pete asked.

"All I had to do was set this meeting up. The rest is up to you and your boy. Since he's not here I'm assuming that you're going to speak for the both of y'all?"

"Yeah, we're in this equally."

"So, what do you think?" Will asked.

Pete looked at him confused. "What do I think about what?"

Will chuckled. "I'm not talking to you. I'm talking to him." He nodded his head towards a wall. The wall slid open and Pete reached for his gun, but stopped when he saw Will shake his head.

"I wouldn't do that if I were you."

"You should listen to him. I don't react well with a weapon pointed at me." A big Russian man said as he stepped into the room with them. The wall closed back when he did.

"Oh, I see y'all on some next level shit around here." Pete said as he relaxed a little.

"I'm Alexei Romanov."

"You're Russian?"

Alexei chuckled as he walked over to the bar. "Yes, I am. I've done my research on you and your friend as well."

"So do we check out?"

Alexei made himself a drink and gulped it down before making another one. "Yes, you do. I like your work ethic and how you handle business. We would need to do a test run first though."

"We can do that. With your pure dope and our work ethic this could be a great business move for all of us."

"I agree with you on that."

Will stood up and walked over to the bar. He poured three shots and handed one to each man. "Let's drink to the start of a good business relationship."

Alexei smiled. "You've been learning how Russians start and end a business meeting I see."

Will chuckled. "You know I'm a quick learner."

They all gulped down their shot of vodka and then placed the shot glass on the bar. Alexei turned to Pete and reached out his hand. Pete took it and shook it.

"Tomorrow we will discuss the rest of the details. Enjoy Chicago; it's a beautiful city." He said.

"Should I be expecting a call with the time and place?"

He nodded. "Yes, Will is going to handle all of that." Alexei then stared at them for a minute.

"Have anyone ever told you that you two favor each other?"

Pete and Will glanced at each other and shook their head. "No."

"You should look into that." He said before he turned around and left out the same way he came in.

A few minutes had passed since Alexei left. "Is this your first time in Chicago?" Will asked.

"No, I've been here a few times. This is just my first time here on business."

Will nodded. "Was that your first time hearing the name Romanov?"

"No, in this business everyone should know that name. It is the first time seeing one of them though. How did you get into business with them?" Pete asked as he put his hands in his pockets.

"A man that was like a father to me put me in contact with one of them. Long story short, after that we became close and soon I was in good with the whole family."

"Damn, you had lucked up. I heard that's a family you don't want to be an enemy of."

Will chuckled. "All the rumors you've heard about them are true."

Pete was about to speak again, but the ringing of Will's phone stopped him. Will answered it on the third ring.

"I hope you're calling to tell me that you're back on Chicago soil." He said into the phone. He paused for a few seconds.

"Good; I'll meet you at the house, baby." He ended the call and looked at Pete.

"You want to know what else I lucked up on?"

"What's that?"

"I fell in love with one of the deadliest Romanovs of them all." He smirked.

Pete thought about it for a minute and then it clicked. "Cori Romanov... you're fucking... I mean you're dating Cori Romanov."

"The best thing you can do in life Pete is find a woman who understands you. A woman that matches your hustle and ambition. One that won't change who you are, but help you become better." Will smirked at him.

"From that look in your eyes I can tell that you've already found her."

"Yeah, something like that."

"Well, I'll have Zel contact you with the time for tomorrow."

"Thanks for setting this up for us."

"No thanks needed; just handle your business like y'all been doing."

"Bet."

Will let him out of the building. It was something about Pete that had him curious. He needed to do some more digging on him.

~~~~~~~~~~~~~~~~~~~~~~~~~~~

Cori had just gotten back in town from doing a job for Acardi. She felt good being back to her usual self. It was a moment after the bombing that she thought she'll never be the same. As soon as she stepped foot in the house her phone rang.

"Hello?"

"Hey Cori, it's us." Alyona said into the phone.

"Who is us?"

"Me, Katara, and Heidi, duh."

Cori laughed. "It was a rhetorical question, Alyona."

"Oh, shut up." They all laughed.

"What can I help you ladies with today?"

"Well, we wanted to talk to you about the wedding." Heidi said.

"What about it?"

"Have you set a date yet or made any plans for it?" Katara asked.

Cori frowned. "No, I've been a little busy."

"Are you planning on getting married this century or the next?" Alyona questioned causing them to laugh.

"I was going to hire a wedding planner. You know I'm not into all that planning stuff."

"Are y'all doing a long or short engagement?"

"We don't want to wait too long to get married. We're both so busy though so I don't know what date I want. I'm thinking about a Fall or winter wedding, but next year though."

"That sounds nice and what about location?" Heidi asked.

"I don't want a church wedding and I want to get married here in Chicago." Cori replied.

"It sound like you got most of it planned out, boo. I just hope you pick a date where I can get rid of some of this happy weight first." Katara stated.

"She's been getting dick down and don't know how to act. Katara, you look beautiful so stop it." Heidi said.

"Girl, my hips has spread, my ass gotten bigger, and these thighs are too thick. All I do is work, eat, fuck, and repeat. Zel got me out here gaining weight because I forget to add work out to the list."

Cori laughed. "You look great friend and you're happy so don't worry about the weight. If it bothers you too much you can always come work out with me."

"Hell naw!" She shouted. They shared another laugh.

"You said that a little too quick, but I understand it." Alyona giggled.

"Y'all know she do too damn much. She not about to kill me. The first red flag is that she wakes up to work out before the sun could fully hit the sky."

"It's not that bad." Cori chuckled.

"I'll pass love, enjoy."

"You are a mess."

"I'll be that then. I'll talk to y'all later I'm having dinner with Zel and Zela at his house tonight." Katara said. They all said their goodbyes and ended the phone call.

Cori headed upstairs to shower and wait for Will to get home.

~~~~~~~~~~~~~~~~~~~~~~~~~~

Katara finished getting ready and headed out the door. It didn't take her long to get to Zel's house. She parked next to his car in the driveway. She then checked herself out in the mirror one more time before she got out the car.

"You were supposed to be here fifteen minutes ago." Zel said when he opened the door.

"I know, but I wanted to look good for you." She smiled.

He eyed her body in the burgundy dress that she wore. "You always look, baby." He kissed her and then stepped aside so she could walk in the house.

"Katara, you're finally here!" Zela ran up to her and jumped in her arms.

"Hey baby, I missed you."

"I missed you too."

"You two can go wash your hands while I check the food." Zel said as he headed to the kitchen.

Katara leaned down close to Zela's ear. "Your daddy know how to cook, right?"

Zela giggled. "Yes, my daddy is a good cook."

"Oh, okay. You know we're too cute to be eating burnt food girl." That caused Zela to crack up laughing. Katara loved this little girl so much.

"What took y'all so long to wash your hands?" Zel asked them when they made it to the kitchen.

"We had to make sure we look presentable at dinner." Katara said.

"Yeah daddy, we have to look good at dinner."

He shook his head. "I already fixed y'all plates. If you want more let me know."

Everyone took their seats. "This looks good, Zel."

"I hope you like it. It's one of my go to dish that I make for me and Zela."

"Yup, shrimp and chicken alfredo with garlic bread." Zela responded.

"Do you want to say grace, baby girl?"

Zela nodded. "Lord we thank you for this food that we're about to receive. We thank you for the people that are at this table and bringing us all together. Please continue to bless us for we are so very grateful. Amen."

"Amen." Katara and Zel said at the same time.

They had small talk while they ate. Katara couldn't believe how good the food was. She joked with Zel about him cooking for her every day. He responded by saying that wouldn't be a problem. She smiled throughout the rest of dinner. For dessert they had ice cream on top of a warm gooey brownie.

"I am so full. That was delicious."

"Yes, it was good daddy."

Zel smiled at them. "Thank you, ladies."

There was a knock at the front door that had them all looking at each other confused.

"Are you expecting someone?" Katara asked.

"No, I'll be right back."

Zel grabbed his gun that was in a lock box in the hallway closet. When he got to the door he checked the front porch cameras. He sighed and put his gun on his back waist when he saw that it was Nessa; Zela's mother. He opened the door and stood in front of it blocking her view to the inside.

Nessa looked him up and down. Zel had always been fine to her. His smooth chocolate skin, tall muscular frame, and sexy features always did something to her. Every day she regretted cheating on him. She was trying to get him back, but he acted as if he wanted nothing to do with her if it didn't involve Zela.

"You're not going to let me in?" She asked.

"What are you doing here, Nessa?"

"I came here to talk to you about the custody hearing. I think it's time we both stop trying to be childish and work things out just the two of us."

"I'm not the one being childish. I'm just trying to take care of my daughter. She's the only one that matters to me."

Nessa pouted at his words. "I don't matter to you anymore, Zel? We used to be so good together."

He scoffed. "That was before you cheated on me with multiple men."

"I was lonely, Zel! You were always gone and working!"

"Lower you voice and you know damn well that's bullshit. I always made time for you and Zela. You just had your sister and friends in your ear telling you that you should be a hoe like them." He spoke between clenched teeth.

She ignored all that he said and only focused on one thing. She glanced back at the driveway and noticed the second car parked in it next to his. She then looked at him with her head tilted slightly to the side.

"What do I need to lower my voice for? Who do you got up in there? You better not have any bitches around my daughter, Zel!" She shouted trying to make sure whoever it was heard her.

"Get off my doorstep and go home, Nessa."

"No, you got some bitch in there while my daughter is here? Go get my child so I can take her home! You not about to be playing house with my baby!"

Zel pulled the door close behind him as he stepped outside. He got directly in Nessa's face so only she would hear and know what he's saying.

"This is the last time you will play with me. I've let you slide because of you being Zela's mother, but that ends today. You know who I am and what I'm capable of. I'm going to tell you one more time before I get angry and Zela ends up without a mother. Get off of my property and go home. The next time you see my face will be in court when I win full custody of my daughter."

"Zel..."

"You've been warned and I'm not repeating myself again."

Nessa glared at him and stomped off to her car. She got in the driver seat and pulled off.

Zel took a deep breath and relaxed before he went back inside. He heard music coming from the kitchen. He stopped in his tracks at the sight before him. Katara and Zela were listening to music off her phone while cleaning the kitchen. He noticed that the music was turned up loud enough to block out all of the yelling that Nessa was doing. He chuckled a little at them trying to hit the high notes. The smiles on their faces made his heart swell.

"Y'all do know that neither one of y'all can hold a note, right?" He asked getting their attention.

They both looked at him and then at each other before they sung even louder than before. That was their way of telling him not to hate and mind his business. He did just that and helped them finish cleaning the kitchen.

After they finished with the kitchen Zel gave Zela a bath and put her down for bed. Once she fell asleep, he led Katara into his bedroom and locked the door. He sat on the edge of the bed and pulled her to him.

"You know the plan was just for me to have dinner and then go home." She told him with a smile.

Zel pulled on the hem of her dress and started moving it up her thighs. "Plans can change, baby."

He removed her dress from her body and kissed her flat stomach.

"Zel..."

"Yes, baby?"

"Will she be a problem for us?" She asked him.

He looked up in her eyes as she stared down at him. "No."

"Are you sure about that?"

"Yes."

"Okay." She went to remove her heels but he stopped her.

"Leave those on."

She grinned at him. She removed her bra and as soon as her breast were free his mouth was all over them.

While he licked and sucked on her breast he removed her panties. He tossed them across the room and then stood up. He stepped back and admired her beauty for a moment.

"Damn, you are beautiful, baby."

Katara pulled his shirt over his head and undid his jeans. When they dropped to the floor, his boxer briefs were soon to follow.

She smiled as she stared as he beauty long thick dick. It was black and beautiful. She rubbed her hand down his chest.

"How do you want me, baby?" She asked with a purr.

"I want you to get on the bed with your legs spread eagle style for me."

"Will you reward me with something big and long?"

He smirked with a slight chuckle. "I plan to reward you with a mind blowing orgasm."

That had Katara rushing over to the bed. She laid down on her back and spread her legs as wide as they would go. She then watched as Zel walked over to her while stroking his dick. He wasn't worried about a condom because he loved the feel of being inside her with nothing in between them. She was on birth control so she wasn't tripping about it either. Zel climbed between her legs and placed his dick directly at her opening. He didn't immediately put it in. Instead he teased her by sliding it up and down the crease of her pussy lips.

"Baby, please..." She moaned. She could feel herself about to cum just from him rubbing her pussy.

"Please, what baby?"

"Please put it in and make me cum." She begged.

He did just as she had requested. He thrust into her slow and steady at first. His pace increased when he felt her pussy muscles tighten around him.

"Fuck!" He grunted as he pushed in and out of her.

"Ooooh shit, Zel!" She moaned.

He threw her legs over his shoulders and went deeper. He fucked her hard until they both came together. Her body started shaking from the intense orgasm she experienced.

"Damn." She mumbled damn near out of breath.

"Are you okay?"

She looked him in the eyes. "No, I think you broke me." She said with a satisfied smile on her face.

He leaned down and kissed her soft lips. "I'll put you back together then."

Zel removed her shoes and then pulled her into his arms. He knew they needed to shower and change the sheets, but he decided to rest for a minute. He wanted to enjoy the moment they just shared together. Zel wanted many more moments like this with Katara. He was going to do everything in his power to make sure it happened.

Halloween, Thanksgiving, and Christmas flew by like a breeze. They all had a lot to celebrate during the holidays. Zel had finally won his custody battle and got full custody of his daughter. His relationship with Katara was doing well. They had gotten even closer and the love word was on the tip of both of their tongues.

Cori and Will had been talking with doctors about her getting pregnant. Most of them had flat out told her that she would never conceive and give birth to a child. She was crushed, but Will told her that they could always adopt or get a surrogate. It had put her in a sour mood for a while until she spoke with a highly recommended doctor back in Russia. That doctor told her not to give up hope because anything was possible. That put Cori in a better spirit. She decided that once they got married they were going to work on having a baby.

"What are you over there thinking about?" Will asked as they chilled in their inside jacuzzi.

She moved closer to him. "I'm thinking about us."

"Oh yeah? What about us are you thinking about?"

She wrapped her arms around his neck. "I'm thinking about our future and what it could possibly be like. Could you picture little us running around here?"

"Yeah, I can picture them tearing some shit up." He chuckled.

"They won't be that bad."

"Yeah, okay."

"They'll be beautiful and a perfect mix of the both of us."

"I can definitely picture that." He kissed her.

Will's phone going off stopped their make out session for a minute. He reached over for his phone on the side table.

"Hello?"

"Mr. Cooper, I'm sorry to be calling you this late, but I have good news." The private investigator he hired said.

Will sat up a little straighter. "What's the good news?"

"Your suspicions were correct, sir. It's a huge possibility that he's your brother."

"Are you sure?"

"Yes, all the information adds up. A DNA test would farther prove it, but yes I'm sure."

"What's wrong, baby?" Cori asked from beside him.

He looked at her. "I think we found my brother."

Cori smiled at him. She was happy for Will. She knew how much it meant to him to find his brother.

"What's the next move?" She asked.

"Where is he now?" Will asked the private investigator.

"St. Louis; he was born and raised there. That's where he lives."

Will chuckled. "I don't even know why I asked that when I already knew that much. Thanks for everything, man. Your bonus will be transferred to your account within an hour."

"Thank you so much, Mr. Cooper. If you ever need any more help with finding someone just give me a call."

After he ended the call he found Cori still staring at him. "What are we going to do now, baby?"

"We're taking a trip to St. Louis."

"I'll get our bags packed." She climbed out of the jacuzzi and dried herself off before she headed to the master bedroom.

Will followed her while still a little in shocked. "I found him." He mumbled.

~~~~~~~~~~~~~~~~~~~~~~~~~~~~

The following evening Will and Cori had checked into their hotel room. Will was still reeling from the new information the private investigator had told him. Apparently, his brother had been shot. He told him to get all the information on what happened and get it to him. When he got what he asked for he and Cori made some moves. While they were out handling business Will noticed a missed call and message from Zyir. He met him when he came out for the meeting him and Pete had with Alexei after the original one he had with Will. He was curious to why he was calling him now. Any business that needed to be discussed had to go through Alexei. Then it donned on him that he might be calling for the same reason Will and Cori were there.

He returned his phone call after he got settled.

"Hello?"

"I got your message earlier. What is it that you wanted to talk to me about?" Will asked.

"I was hoping we could have this conversation face to face. I could fly out there tomorrow if that's cool with you?" Zyir replied.

"You're in luck then. I'm in your neck of the woods."

"You're in St. Louis?"

"Yeah, I was out here with my lady handling some business."

"Okay cool, can we meet up now and talk?"

"I'm free to do that. Just hit me with the location."

"I'm about to text it to you now."

"Okay, got it. I'll be there in an hour."

Will placed the phone down on the bed after he ended the call. He told Cori the conversation he had just had with Zyir. They took a quick shower together and then left out to go meet up with him.

~~~~~~~~~~~~~~~~~~~~~~~~~~

Zyir stood at the bar in his in home office. He had just finished off one drink and was about to make himself another one when his doorbell rang. He turned towards the monitors to see who it was. When he saw that it was the person he was expecting, he walked out the office.

"Thanks for coming?" Zyir greeted his guest.

"It wasn't a problem. I think we're here to talk about the same reason why I'm in town. Oh and this beautiful lady right here is my fiancé Cori." Will replied as they walked inside the house.

Zyir tried not to look shocked at the fact that Cori Romanov was standing in his home. "It's nice to meet you."

"You have a beautiful home, Zyir." Cori said as she glanced around as he led them to the living room.

"Thank you, but that credit goes to my wife."

"Well, she has great taste."

"Okay, let's get down to business. I want to know if what you want to talk about matches what I want to talk about." Will said to Zyir as they all took a seat.

"What did you want to talk about?"

Will smiled. "You go first."

"Since your stomping grounds is in Chicago, I was hoping you could help me find someone."

"Who?"

"It's a man by the name of Gary Cooper. It's very important that I find him." Zyir said.

"That won't be possible." Will told him.

"Why?"

"Because the Gary Cooper that you're looking for died a few months ago from alcohol poisoning and liver failure." Cori said.

"How do you know that's the one I'm looking for?"

"We know because you're looking for the one that fathered Pete. That's the one and he's dead."

Zyir looked at Will for a minute after he said that. "How do you know all that?"

"I know because I did my research. When I first met Pete and saw how similar we looked I did some digging. Gary Cooper is also the man who fathered me. He and my mother was married. I left home at fifteen due to Gary and his bullshit and never looked back. Well, until the day I saw Pete. I found Gary and asked him if he had any more kids. He told me that he had knocked up some chick name Patrice that lived in St. Louis."

"Damn." Zyir said as he started putting all the pieces together.

"So, you knew that you and Pete were related for months now?"

Will nodded his head. "Yeah, I just didn't know how to approach him about it. I mean, Gary never did shit for me either, but I don't know how Pete would react. Gary didn't even claim him."

"Why are you here now?" Zyir asked.

"I'm here because I heard that my little brother needs a liver transplant. I got tested already and found out that I was a match. I'm here to donate part of my liver to him." Will explained.

Zyir jumped up. "Are you serious right now?"

"Yes, I'm serious. There wasn't any way that I was going to let my brother die with knowing that I could help him."

"Damn, I don't know what to say."

Zyir turned towards the hallway when he heard the front door open. A few seconds later he heard tiny little feet running.

"Daddy, we're here!" The twins shouted and ran towards him.

"Hey babe, who car is that in the..." Brittany stopped talking when she saw that Zyir wasn't alone.

"Hello." She greeted the guest.

"Hello." They both replied.

"Baby, this is Will and Cori. Will is Pete's brother and..."

"Me and Malia's cousin. Oh my God, you found him!" She shouted with excitement.

Will looked at Zyir confused about what his wife said. "Who is Malia and how would Pete being my brother make us cousins?"

Brittany decided to answer the question for him. "Well, if you're Pete's brother that means Gary is your father..."

"Correct." Will agreed.

"Gary is my mom and Malia's mom's brother. Which makes us cousins."

Cori looked at him and smiled. "It's a small world, huh? You have family out here."

"Yeah, I guess I do."

"Wait, if you're here in St. Louis, does that mean you're going to help Pete?" Brittany asked.

"Yeah, I'm going to donate." Will replied.

"Yessss! Have you told Pete and Darla yet?" She asked Zyir.

"No, I just got the news myself. I'll wait to tell him in the morning it's been a long day for them. Plus, I'm sure Will want to have an one on one talk with him."

"Yeah I do so the morning sounds good."

"Have y'all eaten dinner yet?" Brittany asked.

"No, we haven't eaten yet. We were going to try to find a restaurant when we left here." Cori answered.

"How about you guys stay for dinner?"

"Naw, we don't want impose." Will said.

"Y'all won't be." Zyir said as he picked Zanden up out of his car seat.

Briya and Briana walked over to Will and stood in front of him. They were looking up at him smiling.

"You look like our Uncle Pete." Briya said.

"Yeah, you really do." Briana nodded in agreement with her sister.

"Fair warning, they really love their Uncle Pete. They might not let you up out of here now." Brittany laughed.

"They're so beautiful and your son is a handsome little guy." Cori complimented.

"Thank you... are they cute enough to get y'all to stay?"

Cori and Will laughed. "Yes, we'll stay for dinner." Will said.

"Yesss! Come on we'll show you our toy room." The twins both grabbed one of his hands.

"Do you need company in the kitchen?" Cori asked Brittany.

"Sure, Come on girl."

Zyir carried Zanden as they followed the girls and Will to their toy room. This would give him a good opportunity to fill Will in about Pete. He felt a huge relief knowing that his boy was going to be okay.

~~~~~~~~~~~~~~~~~~~~~~~~~~~~~

The following morning Zyir and Brittany met Will and Cori up at the hospital to see Pete. When they walked into the room Darla was seated on the bed with him. Pete was kissing on her neck while she just kept giggling and moving his hand away from her thighs.

"Stooop babe."

"Why you being stingy, sexy?" He asked her as he kissed her neck.

"Look at you; you only been up twenty-four hours and already trying to be nasty." Brittany said catching their attention.

"Britt, she being stingy so I can't even be nasty like I want to."

Darla climbed out of the bed. "I was just going to call and tell y'all the good news." She said.

"We came to tell you some good news too. You go first?" Brittany said.

"The doctors came in this morning and told us that they have a donor for Pete." Darla squealed with excitement.

"That's what we came to tell you too."

"Wait, how did y'all know already?"

"What's going, Zyir?" Pete asked as he glanced at Will and Cori.

"Will wanted to come up here and talk to you before the surgery. He's the one donating part of his liver to you." Zyir explained.

"Why would you do that? I mean, I'm not being ungrateful or anything. I'm thankful that you're doing it. I just want to know why?" Pete asked.

Will took a step towards the bed until he was directly next to it. He looked Pete square in the eyes. "I'm doing it because I have no plans of letting my brother die. I was hoping when this is all over we could get to know each other." He told him.

"Wait, your Gary's other son?"

"Unfortunately, yes. There isn't much to know about him. He was a weak excuse for a man."

Pete nodded. "Are you the only child he had?"

Will smirked and placed a hand on Pete's shoulder. "Apparently, not anymore. I have you for a brother."

Pete smiled. "I agree, when this is over we need to get to know each other."

"Tell him the other part, Will." Brittany encouraged.

Will chuckled. "Apparently, we also have some cousins out here."

"Oh yeah, who?"

"Me! Well, me and Malia. Gary was our moms' brother." Brittany said.

"Damn, the world is really small. I've been around my real blood cousins for years and never knew it." Pete said amazed.

"That's what I told Zyir that you were going to say." Brittany stated.

Pete glanced over at Darla and saw her talking to Cori. They were laughing about something. Pete smirked at the fact his baby was standing in front of one of if not the most deadliest woman on the planet.

"How the hell did you get a Romanov?" Pete whispered.

Will glanced over at his woman and then back at his brother. "That's an interesting story that I'll wait to tell you after you walk out this hospital."

"Okay, deal."

After Zyir and Brittany left the hospital; Will and Cori stayed behind. Pete and Will talked about their upbringing and everything else they could think of about their lives. Darla and Cori got to know each other as well. Only the things Cori felt comfortable with telling her. They got along great.

During the time they spent talking, Pete's doctors came in. They let them know that the surgery was set to happen in two days.

~~~~~~~~~~~~~~~~~~~~~~~~~~~~~

Will and Cori left the hospital and headed straight back to their hotel. After they talked about everything they learned about Pete, they took a shower together. While in the shower Will make love to her. When they got out they laid out on the bed cuddled in each other's arms.

"Are you worried about the surgery?"

He shook his head. "No, are you worried?"

"A little bit." She admitted.

"There is nothing you need to worry about. I'll be fine, baby. It's not really a big surgery for me. It's a big thing for him though. The recovery isn't that long for that type of surgery either. Everything will be fine; I will be fine."

"You better be or I'm going to kick your ass."

"I believe you." He laughed.

"Good."

"I need to call Zel and give him a heads up." He leaned over and grabbed his phone off the nightstand.

"He's going to want to be out here with you. He's not just your body guard, he's your friend."

"I know."

Will made the call to Zel and just like Cori had predicted he was coming to St. Louis. Even though Will tried to tell him that he would be fine, he wasn't trying to hear it. After a while Will gave up arguing with him.

"Zel is coming out here." He told Cori when he ended the call.

She laughed. "I told you."

He rolled over on top of her and kiss her. They ended up making love again before falling asleep in each other's arms.

Chapter 18

Zel started handling his business right after he got off the phone with Will. He needed to make arrangements for Zela while he was gone. Katara came to mind so he called her up. She picked up on the second ring.

"Did you forget something when you called a few minutes ago to say goodnight?" She asked. He could tell that she was most likely smiling on the other end of the phone.

"No, I actually need to ask you a big favor."

"What do you need?"

"I need to head out of town for a few days and I was wondering if you could watch Zela for me. Her nanny is on vacation at the moment."

There was a long pause on the phone before she replied. "Yes, I'll watch her. When are you going to bring her?"

"I'll bring her in the morning before I head to the airport."

"Okay, that would give me some time to plan something for us to do."

"Thank you, I appreciate you doing this for me." He told her.

"It's not a problem, Zel. We're going to have some fun while you're gone." She giggled.

"I don't know if I like the way you laughed when you said that." He chuckled.

"You just handle your business and I got Zela."

"Thanks baby, now get some sleep because Zela could be a handful."

Katara chortled. "That's only with you because she knows how to play you."

"Wait, what she be telling you?"

"Goodnight, Zel."

"Katara..." It was pointless because she had already hung up. He shook his head and smiled.

"That woman is a trip."

~The following morning~

Zel pulled up to Katara's house and turned the car off. Zela was so excited and eager to see Katara that she was out of her booster seat before he could open his door. He helped her out of the car and stared at her.

"How come you're never this excited to see me?" He asked with a smile playing at his lips.

Zela smiled at him and grabbed his hand. "Katara knows how to do hair, nails, and facials the right way. You don't know how to do that stuff that good, daddy. Plus, she's a girl and we talk about girl stuff."

Zel frowned. "What kind of girl stuff?"

"I can't tell you because you're not a girl. It's not stuff that boys need to know, daddy."

They walked up to the door and Zela rang the doorbell. Zel was still staring at Zela suspiciously when Katara opened the door.

"Hey, boo." She greeted Zela with a hug and let her inside.

"What's wrong with you?" Katara asked Zel as she grabbed Zela's overnight bag out of his hand.

"Zela said y'all be talking about girl stuff that I can't know about because I'm not a girl."

Katara gave him an 'okay and?' look. "I don't get what the problem is?"

"I want to know." He said.

She smirked. "Too bad you're not a girl so you can't know." She leaned up and kissed him before shutting the door in his face.

Zel could hear the two of them laughing and giggling on the other side of the door. He checked his watch and headed back to the car. He had a plane to catch, but when he got back in town he'll deal with his two girls.

"My girls..." He thought as he pulled away from the house.

~~~~~~~~~~~~~~~~~~~~~~~~~~~~~~~~~

The next few days went by in a flash. The surgery for both Will and his brother was a success. They didn't have to stay in the hospital for long. The doctors said that they could finish up their healing and recovery at home. Will plan was to rest for another day in St. Louis then head back home to Chicago. Cori and Zel were by his side the entire time. He appreciated both of them more for that.

"What are y'all trying to eat?" Cori asked them.

"It doesn't matter to me as long as it's good." Zel said.

"Yeah, same with me." Will said from his spot on the chaise. They made sure he was comfortable while he sat in the living room area of their hotel suite.

Cori rolled her eyes. "They say women are the ones who can't decide on what to eat." She scoffed.

"Y'all are..." Will and Zel both started to say, but stopped when they saw the look she gave them.

"Never mind."

"Yeah, that's what I thought. I'm going to order soul food."

"That would work."

Will looked over at Zel for a moment. He was staring down at his phone smiling.

"What are you smiling like that at?" He asked.

Zel glanced over at him. "Katara sent me a picture of her and Zela at the mall. They had just gotten some facials or something."

Cori looked at him. "She's happy with you."

He nodded. "I'm happy with her too."

"You do know if you break her heart I would have to kill you, right?"

He looked at her and Will. He didn't know if she was serious or not, but he was leaning more towards her being serious. "I wouldn't have stepped to her if my intentions was to hurt her."

"Good, Katara is a good person. She's been hurt a few times and I don't think her heart can take any more pain. I'm very protective of my friends but more so her the most." She expressed.

"You don't have to worry about me. I'm not in it to hurt her. I love her." Zel admitted.

That confession had Cori and Will both looking at him with smiles. "Have you told her yet?" Will questioned.

"Naw, but I plan to when we touch back down in Chicago."

"I think the feeling might be mutual." Cori told him.

"I hope so." He stared at the picture of her and his daughter. They had the biggest smiles plastered across their face.

~~~~~~~~~~~~~~~~~~~~~~~~~~~~~

"What should we do next now that we got our faces smoother than a baby's bottom?" Katara asked Zela as they walked hand in hand out of the spa.

Zela giggled. "Let's get ice cream."

"That sound like a good plan."

They made their way over to an ice cream store. It had a nice little line, but it wasn't too long. As they waited for their turn to order they both turned at the sound of Zela's name being called.

"Zela, come here!" A lady yelled out as she walked towards them.

"Do you know her?" Katara looked down at Zela and asked.

"That's my auntie Nisha. She's my mom's sister."

"Oh."

When the lady made it over to where they were, Katara noticed that Zela's mom Nessa was with her along with another woman.

"Zela, you didn't hear your auntie calling you? Who is this lady that you're with? Your nanny?" Nessa asked as she glared at Katara.

"No, she's my daddy's girlfriend."

"His girlfriend?" They all three shouted. They were starting to cause a scene.

"Is that a problem for y'all?" Katara asked.

"Where is Zel?" Nessa asked while looking around.

"His whereabouts is none of your concern anymore. Now, if y'all would excuse us we were about to get some ice cream."

Zela held on tighter to Katara's hand. She loved her mother, but she didn't like her very much. She was happy when she got to live with her daddy full time.

"Give me my daughter, I'm taking her with me because I don't know you." Nessa stepped closer to them.

Katara pushed Zela behind her. "You're not taking her anywhere unless Zel says otherwise."

"Bitch, that's her fucking daughter! Let her hand go and give her to her mother!" Nisha yelled.

"Look, don't let my calm demeanor fool you. I will drag all three of y'all if I have to."

"Excuse me, is there a problem over here?" A mall security guard asked.

"Yes, she's trying to take my daughter. I think she's one of those sex trafficking people." Nessa told him.

Katara looked at her shocked and in disbelief. "Are you serious right now?"

The security guard looked at Katara with his hand rested on his waist. "Ma'am, I'm going to ask that you release the little girl."

"No!" Zela yelled at him.

"She doesn't have custody of her. Her father does and she's trying to take her without his permission."

"Ma'am..."

"Is everything okay over here?" A man that looked very familiar to Katara asked. She felt like she had seen him somewhere before.

"Uncle Jesse, my mommy trying to take me." Zela cried to him.

Jesse looked at Nessa and the women she came with. When Nessa saw him she knew that she had messed up. She didn't know that Zel had people watching over Zela and his girlfriend.

Jesse turned to the guard. "She's not to be near her without permission from her father. I think you should remove your hand from your waist before something terrible end up happening."

The security guard swallowed hard and moved his hand. "I just heard the commotion and then this lady mentioned something about sex trafficking." He nodded towards Nessa.

"That is her damn daughter though!" Nisha shouted at them.

Nessa shook her head. "Nisha, leave it alone."

Her sister whipped her head around to look at her. "What do you mean leave it alone? He has some other bitch out here taking care of your daughter."

"We shouldn't of came over here. Let's just get out of here." Nessa turned on her heels and rushed out of the mall. Her friend and sister was behind her confused on what just happened.

The security guard turned to Katara. "Ma'am, I'm sorry about the confusion."

She rolled her eyes at him. He was ready to shoot her without knowing all the facts. That's the reality of being black in America.

"Are y'all okay?" Jesse asked Katara and Zela.

"Where have I seen you before?"

"I work for Will."

It now made a little sense to her. "Were you following us?"

"It's part of my job. I only make myself seen when need be." He replied.

"Oh okay." She turned to look down at Zela.

"Are you okay?"

She nodded. "Yes."

"Do you still want some ice cream?"

"Yes, please."

"Okay, let's get some ice cream then."

After they got their ice cream and sat down at a table Katara pulled her phone out to text Zel.

Katara: Your baby mama just tried to snatch Zela at the mall.

Zel: What? Are y'all okay?

Katara: Yes, Jesse came and defused the situation. Why didn't you tell me that you had a body guard following and watching us.

Zel: I just found out about that myself. I think that's a conversation for your friend. I appreciate it though so I'm not complaining.

Katara: Cori?

Zel: Yeah, she loves you.

That made Katara smile.

Katara: I love her too. We're okay and Jesse is going to follow us home.

Zel: I'm heading to the airport now. I'll be there in a few hours. I love you both.

She stared at the phone and kept reading over his last text. "He loves me?" She smiled to herself.

Katara: We love you too.

After she replied she put her phone down and finished her ice cream. The smile stayed on her face the entire time.

~~~~~~~~~~~~~~~~~~~~~~~~~~~~~

"She really tried to snatch her in a mall full of people?" Will asked in disbelief.

"Yeah, I tried to be easy on her because she's Zela's mom, but she took this shit too far." Zel said as he took his seat on the plane. They were on Will's jet about to head back to Chicago. He wasn't a hundred percent yet, but he told them he'll rest when he got home.

"I can handle it for you." Cori said as she sat next to Will.

Both men looked at her with a raised eyebrow expression.

"What? I won't kill her. I'll just make sure she knows not to try that shit again. Plus, I'm pretty sure she said something foul to Katara. No one disrespects my friends and thinks everything is sweet afterwards. Ask Heidi's ex-boyfriend."

"What happened to him?" Zel asked.

"He's walking around without a penis after he cheated on her with her brother." She said so nonchalantly that it had both men covering their private part.

Cori smirked as she leaned back in her seat and closed her eyes. She knew that they were staring at her, but she didn't care. No one hurt her friends and walk away unscathed.

~~~~~~~~~~~~~~~~~~~~~~~~~~~~~~~

After things had calmed down with Zel and Katara everything was going smoothly. A week ago Katara had received an apology letter from Nessa and her sister. At first she was thrown off by it, but after Zel told her they had a life death experience she figured they were trying to right all their wrongs. She forgave them, but she would never forget what they tried to pull. It could've gone all bad had Jesse not been there to step in.

Katara also thanked Cori for always having her back. She made sure she told her friends that she loved them at least a few times a week. They were all she had other than Zel and Zela and she wanted to let them know that she cared.

Valentine's day was right around the corner and Cori and Will had to catch a flight to a private island for a wedding. It was an island that his cousin Malia owned. Will found out that her husband Kymani was a billionaire. He made his money using his brain and hands. Will couldn't do anything, but respect it.

The wedding they were going to was his brother Pete and Darla's wedding. They wanted a Valentine's day wedding. It was definitely a short engagement since he had just proposed after he got shot. His plan was to propose on Christmas, but that was the day someone tried to take his life.

Will was glad that he made it and was now about to marry his soulmate. He couldn't wait to do the same with his. He and Cori had celebrated their Valentine's day in Italy a few days ago. They both enjoyed themselves even though fifty percent of the trip they were naked.

"Baby, do you have all your stuff packed?" Will asked Cori.

"Yes, I told you that like three times already."

"Yeah, but the first two times you were lying." He kissed her cheek and slapped her on the ass when he walked passed her.

"I wasn't lying I just didn't tell the whole truth."

"It's the same thing as lying smart ass. What are you doing anyway?"

"I'm texting the wedding planner back. She keeps sending me these ugly colors. I'm about to get Katara on her in a minute."

Will laughed. "Don't do that you know she's scared of Katara after the ugly flower arrangement she sent you."

Cori giggled. "I had to apologize to because of how bad she cursed the lady out."

"They were some ugly flowers though."

"I know they were hideous."

"Come on baby, the plane is waiting for us. We need to stop off in Russia first. I have some business with your uncle and then we'll head to the island." Will told her.

"Okay, I'm ready."

After a quick stop in Russia they were back on the plane headed to the island. They were going to land just in time to make the wedding ceremony so they got dressed on the plane. When they landed they headed straight to the ceremony.

It was beautiful to watch Pete and Darla confess their love to one another. There was barely a dry eye in attendance. After the ceremony everyone headed inside the venue for the reception.

"Congratulations little brother."

Pete turned around at the sound of his brother Will's voice. He embraced him in a brotherly hug.

"Thanks for coming, man. I truly appreciate you for showing up."

Will waved him off. "I told you that I would be here for your special day and I meant that." He replied and then kissed Darla on the cheek.

"You look beautiful, Darla."

"Thank you, Will."

"I love that dress, girl. Who designed it?" Cori asked.

"Malia designed it for me."

"Oh, let me go talk to her about making my wedding dress. I'll be right back, babe." Cori said to Will before she disappeared.

"She's been looking for the perfect dress and coming up short. I kept telling her that she needed to get one made just for her." Will stated with a shake of his head.

"You can't tell women anything these days." Pete said.

Darla slapped him on the shoulder. "Oh hush, Pete."

"We haven't even been married an hour yet and she's already abusing me." He shook his head and then dodged another one of her hits.

"See look at her."

Will laughed, patted him on the shoulder, and walked away. "Good luck, little brother." He said over his shoulder as he headed in the direction he saw his baby go.

Once Cori set something up with Malia about her dress, Will pulled her on the dance floor. They danced, laughed, and had a good time with Will's new family. After the reception they went to their villa and admired each other under the beautiful sunset.

Cori was happy and she couldn't wait to share a moment with Will like the one Pete and Darla shared on their wedding day.

Chapter 19

~A few weeks later~

Back in Russia Stepan had been busy with Max's training. Max was a quick learner and hard worker. Stepan was proud of him and he made sure he told him that often. He could tell that Max needed guidance and reassurance that he mattered to the people around him. Stepan and Alexei showed him that they care every chance they got. During some of the training sessions Naya would sit on the sidelines and watch. She wanted to learn too, but Stepan told her that he'll teach her soon. Naya loved that her big cousin Max was staying with them. He was fun to be around and he spoiled her just like her father and uncle Alexei did. They made her feel safe.

The only time she wasn't happy was when Sasha came over to visit. She didn't like her and never would. Sasha always gave her mean looks when no one else was paying attention.

"You're doing great, Max." Alexei said as he stepped into the gym room.

Max was doing hand to hand combat with Stepan. For Stepan to an older gentleman he was quick on his feet and even quicker with his hands. Max was amazed at himself that he was even able to keep up with him.

"Thanks uncle Alexei. He's a tough person to keep up with, but I'm trying. I think soon he'll be too old to take me on." He joked and nodded to Stepan.

"He's cocky just like his cousin Cori." Stepan chuckled.

"I'll be happy if I was just half as good as her."

Alexei patted him on the shoulder. "You're getting there nephew."

"Let's stop early with training for today. I have some business to handle, but tomorrow we're back at it bright and early." Stepan told him.

"Yes sir."

"Is it my turn yet?" Naya asked. She had on her cute little workout clothes that Cori had gotten her.

"How about we work on your punches?" Max grabbed her kiddie boxing gloves and put them on her.

Stepan smiled at them. "I'm going to go shower and then I'll be in my office if you need me."

"Okay." Max and Naya both replied barely paying attention to him.

Alexei followed his brother out of the gym. "He's been doing good since he's been here with you."

"Yes, his school work had even improved. He was struggling in a few subjects, but with the tutor I hired he's doing better."

"Max coming here was a good fit." Alexei stated.

Stepan nodded in agreement. "I think Naya enjoys him being here more than anybody. He spoils her just like the rest of us."

Alexei laughed. "My little niece knows a good thing when she sees it."

"Mr. Romanov, your niece Sasha has just arrived." Sarah announced as they walked pass.

"I'm sure she's here to see her brother. Let her know that he's in the gym."

She nodded and walked away. Stepan headed up to his room to shower while Alexei headed to his office for a drink.

Back in the gym Naya was showing Max her hand movements and foot work. She smiled hard every time he told her that she was doing a good job.

"Whoa, soon you're going to be better than me." He told her.

"Really?"

"Yup, you have to keep practicing."

"Little brother!" They both turned at the sound of Sasha's voice.

Naya rolled her eyes because she was interrupting her time with her big cousin.

"Hey Sasha, what are you doing here?" Max asked as he walked over and grabbed two water bottles out of the mini fridge for himself and Naya.

"I came here to see you. Why are you so sweaty?" She wrinkled her nose up at his appearance. He had on a gray muscle shirt and black basketball shorts. He was covered in sweat from his face to his arms.

Max waved his hand around the gym. "I was training and working out. That should be obvious shouldn't it?"

She rolled her eyes. "So, how much longer are you going to keep this up?"

"What are you talking about?" He walked over to Naya and handed her one of the water bottles.

"Max, I get that you're mad at mommy for leaving, but we should stick together. You, I, and Dante are all we got. My krov', my sem'ya." (We're blood, we're family.)

He twisted his face up at her words. He was confused on what she was saying. "This is our family too, Sasha. What are you talking about?"

She released a loud sigh. "I'm just saying that I think you should come home. Dante and I miss you."

"You can come here to visit me any time. I'm not leaving, I love it here. It feels like a family here. You think that I'm mad about mom leaving and that's not the case at all. She was barely around when she was here. She hadn't been acting like a mother to us for years now. You and Dante were just too busy doing your own thing to notice it."

She threw her head back as if he had just slapped her face. "Are you saying it doesn't feel like family with me and Dante?"

"No, that's not what I'm saying so stop trying to place words in my mouth."

"I'm just saying what you are trying to say."

"See, this is why I don't talk to you about anything. You always try to change people's words around to make yourself seem right and them wrong. I know that you and Dante are my family. I love you guys. I just don't understand why you both always try to make like I have to choose. They're my family too and I love them as well. You sound so much like mom sometimes it's sickening. You need to get help with that before you turn out like her with hatred in your heart."

He walked off and headed towards a door that was connected to the gym.

"Where are you going? We're not done talking."

"I'm going to the bathroom if that's okay with you!"

"Don't be a smart ass, Max!"

He ignored her and walked in the bathroom shutting the door behind him. Max was tired of Sasha coming over there every other day trying to convince him to come home. This was his home now and he wasn't leaving. His life finally seem like it's on the right track and he's not going to let her or anyone else knock him off.

Sasha glanced around the gym with her face scrunched up. When her eyes landed on Naya she gave her a nasty look.

"That outfit looks hideous on you." She commented.

"Not as hideous as your face looks." Naya said and then stuck her tongue out at her.

"You little piece of shit."

"I know you are, but what am I?"

Sasha stepped closer to her. She bent down so that they were eye level with each other. She had a scowl on her face as she glared at her.

"You really think that you're a real Romanov, huh? Let me remind you that you're nothing, but a stupid little orphan who my uncle felt sorry for. No one really loves you they just pretend to love you. Eventually, they'll get tired of looking at your ugly face and give you to some men like the ones who killed your real mommy and daddy. I bet you won't be smiling then when they beat..."

"What the hell did you just say to her?" Max questioned with an angry facial expression plastered across his face.

Sasha's eyes widened as she stood up straight and turned around. "I... I..."

Max looked at Naya and saw that she had tears rolling down her face. "Why would you say something like that to her?"

"I didn't..."

"Yes, you did I heard you."

Naya ran out of the gym crying. Max glared at his sister. "I think you should leave and never come back here."

"You can't tell me..."

"I can and I just did. What do you think uncle Stepan is going to do to you when he finds out what you said to his daughter? Leave Sasha and don't come back around here. I don't know what your problem is, but you need to get yourself together before it gets you killed." Max left out the gym in search of Naya.

Sasha rushed out of the house before anyone else saw her. She was embarrassed that Max had overheard what she said to Naya. She didn't even hear him come out of the bathroom. She knew that she would be getting a call from her uncle and she wasn't too thrilled about it. Sasha just hated how everyone treated Naya like she was so special. It was the same thing they had done with Cori when they were growing up. She hated the attention and praise that they got.

Stepan and Alexei walked out of the office and were headed out of the front door when they heard knocking coming from upstairs. He spotted Sarah headed up the stairs with a butter knife in her hand.

"What's going on?" He questioned.

"Naya locked herself in her bedroom and refuses to open the door. Max and I are trying to get inside to make sure she's okay. I saw her crying when she ran passed me to her room."

Stepan and Alexei followed her up the stairs to Naya's bedroom door. They saw Max talking through the door trying to get her to open it.

"She's not trying to open the door." He said when he spotted them.

"What happened?" Stepan asked him. The last time he seen his daughter she was with Max in the gym smiling and now she's crying. He wanted to know what had happened in that short time.

"Sasha had said some mean and hurtful things to her. I was in the bathroom at the time, but I heard part of it and it was not something you say to a little kid."

Stepan hid the anger that was burning inside him. Everyone knew that he didn't play about his daughters. "Where is your sister now?"

"I put her out and told her not to come back."

He nodded and then knocked on the door. "Naya, open up the door for, papa."

He waited a minute and nothing happened. He placed his ear to the door and didn't hear anything. Now he was worried that she might have done something to hurt herself.

Alexei stepped forward. "Allow me brother." He pulled out a switchblade and picked the lock. The door opened and they stepped inside. They glanced around and didn't see Naya. Then they heard crying and talking coming from the closet.

Inside the closet Naya hid on the floor in the corner. She had a phone to her ear and was telling her big sister everything that Sasha had said to her. Her young mind didn't quite understand the death wish that she was signing for Sasha.

"Then she said that no one loves me and that I was ugly." Naya cried.

"Princess, you are far from ugly. Have you looked in the mirror recently? You are the most beautiful little girl I had ever seen in my life. I love you, Naya. You know that daddy loves you too along with a lot of other people. Sasha is just stupid and jealous because she's ugly inside. When people are ugly inside it starts to show on the outside as well. Then they say or do mean things to others to make themselves feel better."

"I don't know why she's always mean to me. I didn't do anything to her." Her sniffles could be heard through the phone. That only angered Cori more. She tried to keep herself calm while she reassured Naya that she's loved.

"Naya, don't we show you how much we love you?"

"Yes, but Sasha said that everybody pretends to..."

"We're not listening to what Sasha says. She doesn't know what she's talking about. No more crying over things that isn't true. She hates herself and she wants you and everyone else to be miserable with her. We're not going to do that because why?"

"Because she's an ugly stupid person inside."

That got a giggle out of Naya and Cori. "Yes, exactly baby. I'm going to make sure she never says mean things or mess with you again, okay?"

"Okay, I love you."

"I love you too, princess."

The closet door opened and Stepan appeared after moving some clothes out of the way. "Naya, sweetheart is you okay?"

She stood up and nodded her head. "Yes, I'm better now. My sister said that I'm beautiful and that she loves me."

Stepan smiled at her. "We all love you, printsessa." (princess)

"Cori wants to talk to you." Naya handed him the phone.

Alexei picked her up and carried her out of the room with Max and Sarah following behind them. He heard Alexei ask her if she wanted ice cream. She hasn't had dinner yet so her response was a loud yes. Dessert before dinner always seemed to excite her. Stepan could hear the excitement in her voice.

He placed the phone to his ear. "Hello, daughter."

"I'm going to break her jaw and maybe a few other bones as well."

"I was going to have a talk with her..."

"No more talking with her, daddy. I warned Sasha about saying things like that to Naya. She's a hateful person just like her mother. I'm not going to allow her to make my sister have low self-esteem just because she has it herself. Naya is a child and Sasha is an adult. She knows better, but she just doesn't care about anyone but herself."

"When are you touching down here?" Stepan asked.

"I'm headed to the airport now."

"Okay and Cori?"

"Yes?"

"Let her live... it's been enough Romanov blood shed lately."

"She'll be breathing when I'm finished with her. It would be barely, but she'll survive." Cori ended the call before her father could respond.

Sasha had been warned verbally and she didn't listen. It was now time that she be warned physically.

~~~~~~~~~~~~~~~~~~~~~~~~~~~~

She stumbled in the house after a night out with her friends. She had been drinking way too much and was surprised she made it home in one piece. After tossing her clutch purse on the coffee table, she removed her heels.

"These shoes are cute, but they hurt like hell." She complained as she rubbed her sore feet. She glanced around the dark living room. She hadn't seen Dante's car in the driveway so she knew he wasn't home.

"He's probably out fucking one of his many sluts."

She stood up and was about to head to the kitchen when a voice spoke out from the shadows. It had scared her so bad that she ended up pissing on herself.

"Did you think I wouldn't show up after what you did, Sasha?"

Sasha turned around feverishly looking for where the voice came from. "Cori?"

"Hi, cousin." Cori stepped out from out of the shadows.

"I didn't mean..."

Before she could complete her sentence, Cori had sent a swift kick to her chest. Sasha hit the floor hard crying.

"She's a little kid, Sasha. How could you fix your lips to say those things to her?"

"I'm sorry..."

"No, you're not sorry but you will be." She punched her in the face multiple times. Within seconds blood started to cover her face.

"You are just like your hateful mother. She used to try that mess with me when I was a kid too. I had grandma there to protect me. Naya has me to protect her. I'll kill anybody that tries to hurt her. That includes family as well. This is your last warning Sasha. Stay the hell away from my sister or die." Cori sent a hard kick to her ribs. She knew from the impact that at least three of them were broken.

After that Cori left out the same way she came in. She headed straight to the airport strip where the plane was waiting to take her back to Chicago.

Chapter 20

The day was September thirtieth. The weather was perfect for the beautiful occasion. It wasn't too cold and it wasn't too hot; it was just right. The guest had arrived a little over twenty minutes ago and had already been seated. Soft music played in the background as they waited for the ceremony to begin. Everyone was anxious and excited to be there. It was a very private event and not just anyone was allowed to witness what was about to take place. If you were present it meant that you were somebody of importance.

Once the soft music stopped playing and *'Perfect'* by Ed Sheeran began to play, all of the guest turned their head towards the entrance. Will lead the way down the path to the flowery arch with his groomsmen behind him. His groomsmen consisted of Zel, his brother Pete, Max, Jason, and Jesse. Each man wore a black three piece tuxedo with a red handkerchief in the chest pocket.

After the groomsmen took their place the ring bearer made his way down next. Kian smiled at all the guest as he carried the pillow that held both rings on it. He had no idea that he was carrying millions of dollars in his hands.

When he made it to the front the music switch to *'All of Me'* by John Legend. One by one the bridesmaids made their way down. Cori had more bridesmaids than Will had groomsmen. That's why they chose for everyone to walk down one by one instead of paired up. The bridesmaids' dresses were all the same in color and length. It was a black a line princess one shoulder floor length chiffon dress with a ruffle.

Malia, Brittany, Tari, Monica, Heidi, Katara, and Alyona each held a single red rose in their hand. Naya and Zela were the next ones to walk down. They both wore pretty white flower girl dresses. Their hair had one ponytail at the top side of their head with the rest of the hair in curls down in the back. They strolled down side by side while tossing red and white rose petals on the ground.

Everyone stood to their feet and faced the entrance when *'Die with You'* by Beyoncé started to play. Cori stood at the beginning of the path in a beautiful off the shoulders floor length mermaid red lace dress.

"Are you ready, ˈānjəl?" (angel)

She glanced up at her father. "I've never been more ready for something in my life."

"Nu, togda davay pozhenimsya." (Well, let's get you married then.)

Stepan walked his daughter down to her future. It was a bittersweet moment for him. He was happy to be there and share in the moment with her.

Cori was so breathtaking that Will had to take deep breaths to calm himself down. He bit down on his bottom lip to try and keep the tears that threatened to escape his eyes at bay. His future; his everything was walking towards him and he felt overwhelmed by the blessing he was given.

"She's all yours, son." Stepan told him after he kissed Cori's cheek.

Will shook his hand and then stared at Cori. She smiled at him with that beautiful smile that always sent his heart into a frenzy.

"You look absolutely gorgeous." Will told her.

"You're looking very handsome yourself."

"Are you ready to join me forever?"

Cori grinned. "You were already stuck with me forever."

They both turned towards the reverend with huge smiles on their faces. Will and Cori expressed their feelings for each other through their vows. It was raw, uncut, and beautiful.

After they said their 'I do' everyone stood to their feet and clapped for the newlyweds. Will had swooped his new wife up in his arms and carried her down the flowery path.

"I wonder if they're going to make it to the reception." Alyona commented causing everyone in earshot to laugh.

~Two hours later~

Cori and Will did manage to make it to their reception, but they were forty minutes late. When they walked in everyone had laughed and joked with them about being freaks. They had spent time with their friends and family. They danced, laughed, and ate cake.

Everyone gathered outside when it was time for the bride and groom to leave. They had a black limousine waiting for them. The limo was going to take them straight to the plane so they could head off to their honeymoon.

"Where are you guys going for your honeymoon?" Tari asked them.

"We're going to Greece for a little bit and then Italy for like a week." Cori replied.

"Well you two have fun and enjoy being husband and wife."

Cori smirked at Will. "Oh, I'm going to enjoy him."

All her girls laughed as they gave her a hug. Will then walked over to her and grabbed her hand.

"Are you ready, baby?"

"Yes, I'm ready."

As they walked to the limousine hand in hand Cori spotted Acardi. She smiled and winked at him. He returned her look with a smirk.

Everyone waved when Cori and Will got into the limo. When it pulled off they all started to head back inside. The party was still going.

A minute later they all turned and screamed when they heard a loud explosion. When they looked down the street they saw that the limo that Cori and Will had gotten in was now in flames.

Stepan's eyes widened as he ran down the street to the explosion. He was so focused on trying to make sure if his daughter and Will were okay; he didn't realize that others were running with him. When they made it to the limo it was too much smoke and flames for any of them to get near it.

Stepan dropped down to his knees as he looked at it. A piece of his heart and world was in that limousine and now it was gone. Alexei placed a hand on his brother's shoulder as he stared at the burning vehicle.

Tari and her parents were in just as much shock as Stepan was. Will was her brother and best friend. She had already lost so much. She didn't know if her heart and sanity could take another major loss like this.

"Noooo!" She screamed as tears poured from her eyes.

"Who did this? Kto eto sdelal?" (Who did this?) Stepan shouted. You could hear the pain in his voice.

Zel made it down to the explosion after he got the kids inside safely. He glanced around and saw everyone in a panic. It was starting to feel like the bloodshed would be never ending. Chicago was once again about to be a war zone.

~~~~~~~~~~~~~~~~~~~~~~~~~~~

It had been three weeks since Cori and Will's death. Stepan stayed in Chicago for the first week trying to find out what happened. When he didn't get the results he wanted he had gone back to Russia with Naya. She had completely shut down on everyone. She hadn't spoken since the wedding. All she did was nod or shake her head when asked questions. She and Stepan were both taking Cori's death hard.

Stepan had started to drink a lot more than he used to. Max was worried about his uncle, but more importantly he was worried about Naya. He wanted to do something to help her so he called the one person he felt could lend him a hand.

"Thanks for coming, uncle Alexei."

Alexei waved his hand. "No need to thank me. You said that you needed help with something. What is it?"

Max hesitated for a second. "I don't know how to say this without overstepping."

"Just open up your mouth and let it out."

"I think that uncle Stepan is having a mental meltdown. He's been kind of losing it since the funeral we had for Cori and Will. He's been drinking a lot more and not being the strong man that he is. Naya needs him right now, but he's no help to her. I was hoping that if it was okay with you that I take Naya to visit aunt Sofia. We could stay the weekend and see if she could help with Naya. Then maybe you could help uncle Stepan. I don't know how to help him."

Alexei smirked at him. "You're helping him now by coming to me. I'll make the arrangements for you and Naya to go to my home with Sofia. She's been asking to see our niece anyway."

"Thank you."

"You're growing up to be an outstanding young man, Max. Never change who you are no matter who tries to persuade you."

Max nodded and then headed upstairs to pack his and Naya's stuff. After he was done he found Naya in her toy room. She was seated at her mini table staring out of the window.

"Naya, do you want to go to visit aunt Sofia?"

She shrugged her shoulders and continued to stare out of the window. Max walked closer to her.

"Aunt Sofia had been asking about you. She misses you a lot and really wants to see you. Do you miss her, Naya?"

She nodded. "Would you like to go see her? I'm sure she's waiting to bake cookies and brownies with you like you two used to."

She nodded her head again. "Okay, let's put your shoes on and go."

Naya allowed him to help her put her shoes on. When he was done she stood up and grabbed his hand. Sarah stopped them outside the room door.

"Your uncle Alexei told me that I would be accompanying you and Naya to his house."

"Okay, well I had already packed her things. All you have to do is pack yours and then meet us down at the car."

"Okay." She headed to her bedroom to get her things together.

Stepan stood in the window with a bottle of vodka in his hand. He watched as the car that held the last piece of his world and heart pulled out of the circular driveway. He wanted to be a better man for Naya; a better father. He just had to rid the world of the person responsible for taking her sister from them first.

Alexei walked over and stood by his brother. He had a drink in his hand. After he watched the car disappear out of their sights, he spoke to his brother without looking at him.

"This family has been through a lot within a short timeframe. We had withstood some of the toughest challenges together. This won't be any different."

"I won't rest until the person responsible for this is dead and in a shallow grave."

"It will be done, brother. We'll make sure of it like we always do." Alexei stated. On that they both took a drink.

~~~~~~~~~~~~~~~~~~~~~~~~~~~~~~~~

Later that night the house was completely silent. Stepan was in the den room asleep in front of the fireplace with a half empty bottle of vodka in his hand. Alexei had gone up to bed over an hour ago. The reflection of the flames from the fire dance across Stepan's face.

A dark shadow crept into the room. For a few minutes they stood off in the corner and watched Stepan.

With a knife at their side in one hand and a gun in the other they started to move towards him. They stopped dead in their tracks when a voice they weren't expecting spoke to them.

"Do you know that he didn't want to believe me when I told him it was you that was behind everything? That's why I had to put on a little show to prove it to him. He's a very stubborn man as you know." Cori said with a sneaky grin spread across her face.

Stepan stood up from his spot on the chair. He glared at the person that had been behind all of the attacks since Alyona's wedding.

"I see you are more like your mother than I thought."

"I thought you were passed out drunk?" Dante asked him.

"I bet you thought a lot of things. Did you really think that you could kill my daughter and her husband with a car bomb? We've been around for a while and know how to check for those type of things."

Dante glared at him and then at Cori. "Did you know he killed my mother? His own sister and had the nerve to take my little brother in like he's not the reason he doesn't have a mother anymore!"

That's when Alexei made his presence in the room noticed. He had been in there thirty minutes before Dante had snuck into the house. He would've thought that Dante was smart enough to notice something was off when he was able to ease in the house without an issue. They had made it easy for him by disarming the security system.

"Your mother tried to kill his daughter. She was out to spill Romanov blood for a vendetta that was aimed at the wrong person." Alexei sneered.

Dante glanced over at him. "She thought he had killed the man she loved!"

"You know about that, huh?" Cori asked.

He smirked at her. "I know a lot of things. I didn't at first, but over time I learned enough. I knew that Adrian wasn't my real father and he was the one who killed my father."

"Then you killed him in that fake car accident." Alexei said.

"Yes, he deserved it for killing my father. After I found out who my real father was I got in contact with my half-brother. He didn't want any parts of this, but he did lend me a hand by getting me in contact with some Italian shooters for hire. They were the ones who were supposed to shoot at you at grandma's funeral. You ended up getting to them first though."

"You whine about my father taking your mom from you and your siblings, but you killed their father. You are the one who made Max an orphan." Cori shook her head.

"My mom was misguided because of him!"

"Your mom was a whore that got what she deserved." Cori spat.

Dante went to aim his gun at her, but Alexei was quicker than him. Alexei took three quick steps and swung the blade that was in his hand. Dante's hand still gripping the gun dropped to the floor.

"Ahhhhhhhh! Moya ruka, ty otrubil moyu ruku!" (My hand, you chopped off my hand!)

He dropped the knife in his other hand so that he could try to stop the bleeding. He started to get light headed and dropped down to his knees.

"Tell me something Dante. What did our grandmother ever do to you for you to kill her?"

He shook his head. "It was an accident. I didn't mean for her to die." He confessed.

"I guess we're even now." Stepan said as he raised the gun he had been holding at his side.

"No, we're not even yet. You meant to kill my mother. Me killing yours was an accident." Dante glanced at Cori.

"She was supposed to be dead, but that's okay. At least I'll die knowing you loss one of your daughters. Cori, I guess you're not always there to protect Naya." He laughed.

"Ughhh!" She ran up and kicked him in the face.

"You finish him off while I go to Naya."

"She's at my house asleep last time I checked in with Sofia." Alexei said.

"I told Sasha that I was always going to protect Naya. She's the only one I said that to. He sent Sasha to kill Naya. They were in on this the whole time!" She rushed out of the house.

Dante started laughing harder with a mouth full of blood. "She'll never make it in time. Naya is probably already died and no one realized it yet."

Stepan shot him right between the eyes. It was the same spot he shot his mother in.

"I'll call the cleanup crew and then we can head to my house." Alexei stated as he stared down into Dante's lifeless eyes.

~~~~~~~~~~~~~~~~~~~~~~~~~~~

When Cori got to her uncle's house she was about to walk up to the door when it came open. Her aunt Sofia stood there with silent tears streaming down her face. She wasn't shocked to see Cori because she had knowledge to the plan beforehand.

"Where is she?" Cori asked in a panic.

"She's in there..." Sofia pointed to one of the rooms down the hall.

Cori ran to the room and stopped dead in her tracks. She took in everything that she was seeing. Naya sat beside Max on the floor with her small arms wrapped around his neck as they both cried. When Max saw Cori in the doorway he wiped the tears from his eyes.

"I had to do it. She was going to kill her. I couldn't let her kill her." He cried.

Cori stepped over Sasha's lifeless body as she lay dead on the floor. A puddle of her blood started to spread out from underneath her. Cori kneeled down in front of Max and removed the gun from his hands.

"Everything is going to be okay."

"I thought you were dead?"

Naya smiled at him. "She wasn't dead we were just pretending so she could surprise someone." She said for the first time in weeks. Naya looked at her sister.

"Did you surprise them? Were they happy to see you?"

"I did surprise them but I don't think they were happy to see me though."

"That's okay, I'm happy to see you. Did I do well with keeping your secret?"

"You did great, princess." Cori picked her up and carried her out of the room. She looked back at Max.

"Come on Max, let's get you two home."

"I'm so confused right now."

"That's okay, you'll learn the truth tonight and it would be your decision on what you do next."

He nodded and then followed them out of the room. That night when Stepan and Alexei arrived they explained everything to Max. They left out no details so that he would be able to choose his next move. After finding out the truth Max was shocked and hurt. He mostly blamed his mom and Dante for all the trouble they caused. It was because of their selfish and hateful thinking that their family had just gone through a civil war.

A week later Max asked his uncles if they could change his last name to Romanov. He was never really close to his Petrov side of the family anyway. They had agreed and just like that he was Max Romanov.

Cori made sure to keep in touch with Max. They talked almost every day on the phone. She wanted to make sure that his sister being his first kill didn't affect him in a negative way. He seemed to be doing fine, but she made sure her father paid close attention to him. Things for the Romanov family had finally started to calm down.

~Epilogue~

After everything that had gone down within the last month Cori and Will was finally able to go on their honeymoon. Their first stop was in Thessaloniki. A city located in Greece on the Thermaic Gulf of the Aegean Sea. They had been there for a few days so far. Cori loved the scenery of the place more than anything else. Will decided to rent out a hot air balloon so that they could have breakfast in the sky. Cori wanted to watch the sunrise from the sky so her husband made it happen.

"It is so beautiful up here."

"Not as beautiful as the woman I'm up here with, but it's okay." He wrapped his arms around her waist from behind and kissed her neck.

"Did you ever think that we would be here right now?"

"Yes, you keep forgetting that I was the one who always knew we would be together. You were the one tripping." He chuckled when she hit him on the arm.

"You are never going to let me forget that are you?"

"Nope, I'm going to be telling our great grandkids that one day. They're going to ask me to tell them about our love story and I'm going to be like, you know your nana tried to run off on me one time. She was acting like she wasn't in love with me and shit."

Cori threw her head back and laughed. "Then I'm going to have to tell them that their grandpa is just crazy and making up stories."

Will chuckled. "You know I love you, right?"

"Yes, I know and I love you too."

"I know we've been trying hard to get pregnant and it's hard. I was thinking maybe we should check out one of those fertility places. What do you think?"

Cori shook her head. "There's nothing wrong with us, Will. We don't need to check that out."

He turned her around to face him. "I know there isn't anything wrong with us, baby. I'm not saying that we're broken or anything. That's not what that's about. Those types of places are very helpful for people who are struggling to have kids."

"I know that..."

"Then are you willing to try it out?"

"No, we don't need..."

"Cori, baby..."

"Just listen to me, baby. We don't need to check it out because we're already pregnant."

He stared at her in shock for a moment before a smile graced his face. "Are you saying that we're going to have a baby?"

"Yes, we're going to be parents!" Her eyes widened at that revelation. It was the first time she had said it out loud. It was one thing to try for a baby, but when it actually happens it was a complete indescribable emotion.

"Damn, I got the woman and now I'm about to get the baby too? The blessings just keep coming."

"Even with all the bad that we do, we're obviously doing something right." She told him.

"I believe that wholeheartedly."

Cori grinned at him. "You know if that man wasn't standing over there controlling this balloon I would sex you right here."

"In a hot air balloon, in the sky, doing the sunrise?" He raised an eyebrow.

"Yup."

"Shiiiiit, you want me to tell him to turn around and close his eyes?"

She shook her head while she laughed hard at him. "No babe, we can wait until we get back to the hotel."

Will turned to the guy behind them. "Aye, you can start heading back now. We need to go celebrate at the hotel. She's having my baby."

Cori covered her face as the man smiled and congratulated them. "You are something else."

"I know I am, but we're actually about to add another Cooper and Romanov to the world. That shit is mind blowing. I know your last name is Cooper now, but you'll always be a Romanov and so will our kids. I respect that."

Cori couldn't do anything but smile at her husband. She was happy to have a man like him in her life. One that took her for who she was and didn't try to change her. She was a Romanov through and through. Their reign of power, love, and loyalty knows no bounds when it comes to protecting what's theirs. The Romanov reign would live on for many years to come.

~Konets.~ (The End.)

Full Length Novels

Written By the

Author

Between Love & Justice

Between Love & Dishonor

Altar'd: A Kalil And Chanae Between Love Novel

The Williams Boys: A Zahyir And Qadir Between Love Novel

Williams Clan: Us Against The World

Amour: Surreptitious Lovers

Mama Didn't Raise Me

Ahdon

Made For Me: Darnell And Lorrisa Story

His Queen: Royal Amante

Her King: Royal Amante

Ambitious: Love & Hustle

Ambitious: Love & Forgiveness

Ambitious: Love & Triumph

Ambitious: Love & Family NYE Novella

Ambitious: Love & Family The Retreat

Wherever Love Takes Me

Pretty Assassin: The Beauty Mark

Choices He Made

He Chose Me: Malik and Kylis

Choosing You: Zyir and Brittany

Romanov Reign

Chosen For Me: Pete and Darla

We Chose Love: A Valentine's Day Novel

Promises Of The Heart

Promise Me Your Heart

Contact Info:

Facebook: Danielle Grant or Author Danielle Grant

Goodreads: Danielle Grant

Instagram: Zanni930

AllAuthor: Danielle Grant

Made in the USA
Middletown, DE
12 December 2024